"You're one hell of a man, Noah Reed."

"And you're one fascinating woman, Brianna Delgado."

She studied his mouth, the way the very corners curled up, even when he wasn't smiling. She'd thought about kissing that mouth more times than she'd admit, even to herself. But taking that first step, the one that could lead to so many others or to no more at all, was complicated.

Noah lifted a hand to her temple, his fingers brushing her curls in a way that was almost erotic. She closed her eyes and luxuriated in the sensation, trying to stay with it instead of wondering where his fingers would touch her next.

His other hand went to her waist, paused a moment, then slid to the small of her back. It remained there, holding her with just the smallest amount of pressure, as if to keep her from floating away from him.

RESOLUTE AIM

—

Leslie Marshman

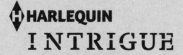

INTRIGUE

For my brother, Scott
Here's to laughing at private jokes until we cry,
crying over shared grief until the tears stop falling,
loving with an unbreakable bond until forever.
From M&DFC to M&DOC with love.

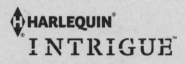

ISBN-13: 978-1-335-58257-7

Resolute Aim

Copyright © 2023 by Leslie Marshman

Harlequin Enterprises ULC
22 Adelaide St. West, 41st Floor
Toronto, Ontario M5H 4E3, Canada
www.Harlequin.com

Printed in U.S.A.

Multi-award-winning author **Leslie Marshman** writes novels featuring strong heroines, the heroes who love them and the bad guys who fear them. She called Denver home until she married a Texan without reading the fine print. Now she lives halfway between Houston and Galveston and embraces the humidity. When Leslie's not writing, you might find her camping at a lake, fishing pole in one hand and a book in the other. Visit her at www.lesliemarshman.com, www.Facebook.com/lesliemarshmanauthor, www.Instagram.com/leslie_marshman or @lesliemarshman on Twitter.

Books by Leslie Marshman

Harlequin Intrigue

The Protectors of Boone County, Texas

Resolute Justice
Resolute Aim

Scent Detection

Visit the Author Profile page at Harlequin.com.

CAST OF CHARACTERS

Noah Reed—Noah became a deputy when his father was still Boone County sheriff, and he's determined to be taken seriously. But the occasional lapse in rule-following and his offbeat sense of humor in stressful situations are holding him back. Instead of taking lead on their latest big case, he's stuck partnering with the new deputy.

Bree Delgado—She resigned as a San Antonio cop to accept a slower-paced deputy position in Boone County. But Resolute isn't the quiet, sleepy town she'd been hoping for. Can she keep her real reason for quitting the big-city force a secret?

Cassie Reed—A stickler for following protocol, she's been sheriff since her father died in the line of duty. She barely has time to welcome Bree before leaving town for a trial. Will having Noah partner with the new deputy prove he can lead an investigation?

Adam Reed—Oldest of the Reed brothers, he's Cassie's chief deputy and in charge while the sheriff is out of town.

Rachel Miller—A waitress at the Busy B Diner, which the Reeds frequent. She befriends Bree, helps her find a place to rent and tries to play matchmaker for her.

Chapter One

Boone County Deputy Noah Reed sat parked just north of town, sighing with pleasure at the first bite of his breakfast sandwich. County patrol, his least-favorite activity, always seemed twice as boring on Mondays.

After leaving a note in the office that he was skipping the morning briefing, he'd grabbed breakfast at the Busy B Café and headed out to enjoy it while it was hot.

He set the cheesy egg-and-bacon delight on the dash and picked up his travel mug of steaming hot, extra-double-strength coffee. It was halfway to his mouth when a deafening explosion caused the mug to slip through his fingers.

Sending up a quick prayer of thanks that the lid was closed and his boys weren't scalded, he fumbled the mug into his cupholder and peered through the windshield. Like the fires of Armageddon, towering plumes of orange and yellow flames surged above the tree line. Black smoke billowed into the cold January sky, bruising the azure dawn. As Noah stomped on the gas pedal, he flipped on his lights and siren, then keyed his mic.

"Helen, this is Noah. We've got an explosion northwest of town in the Rosemont neighborhood." He careened around a corner and followed the smoke to a house engulfed in flames. How many people were trapped inside that inferno?

Powering down his window, he choked on acrid fumes moving in the strong breeze. A cross between the sweet scent of ether and the stench of rotten eggs made his gut churn.

"The 3000 block of Boxwood Lane," he continued, "just west of Barton Road. Requesting backup, along with fire, ambulance and hazmat. Inform everyone that ventilator masks are required. Smells like a meth house. Over."

"Copy. Dispatching fire, ambulance and hazmat to your location." Helen Gibson—the Boone County sheriff's administrative assistant, department dispatcher and de facto mother to all the Reeds—remained as calm and in control as she expected Noah to be. "Sheriff's on her way with backup and masks."

"Copy."

"Noah, you stay sharp."

"Yes, ma'am."

Like a scorching rain, embers showered down on the closest homes, and flaming debris landed in the front yards, igniting small fires in the dry, winter-dead grass. Noah parked several houses away and leaped from his vehicle, his sole mission to make sure everyone was okay. He ran toward the burning home but stopped short as a wall of heat smacked into him. If anyone was in that house, they were beyond his help now.

He turned and took a quick survey of the area.

At least a dozen residents, torn from their homes by the explosion, stood across the street like a horde of stunned zombies and watched the conflagration. Noah raced over to them.

"Y'all need to get inside. These fumes you're smelling are dangerous." When they didn't move, he raised his voice and yelled, "Everybody, inside your homes *now*—windows closed! And keep your pets in there with you!"

An older couple started across the street to a house next door to the destroyed one. Noah ran after them. "You need to stay over there—" he nodded his head toward the direction they'd come and herded them back "—until the fire department says it's safe." He eyed the group who still loitered outside. "Are you friends with anyone out here? Someone you can stay with until the all clear is given?"

A gaunt woman wearing a coat over her nightgown shuffled over to the couple. "Y'all can wait in my house. I'll put on some coffee." She motioned for them to go on in, then turned back to Noah. "Lord have mercy." Her birdlike eyes darted from the destruction across the street to Noah, then to what looked like a decapitated porcelain angel she clutched against her chest. "What is this world coming to?"

After confirming all the residents had retreated inside, Noah turned to her. "Did you see anything happen this morning before the explosion, ma'am?"

"Their comings and goings don't usually start this early." The woman shook her head. "But I'll tell you one thing, don't go getting yourself hurt over the likes of them. Nothin' but druggies in there."

"You know that for a fact?" Noah's gaze swung from the woman to the house and back.

She gave a sharp nod, eyes on the fire. "Everyone on the street knows it. Shady-looking people going in and out at all hours of the night. You learn the signs. It was never like this when the Smiths owned that place, I can tell you that." Finally looking away from the old Smith house, she inclined her head toward Noah, her voice low as if conspiring with him. "At bingo the other night, I heard there's more of them drug houses poppin' up all over the county."

The wind shifted, and Noah grew more concerned about the old woman. "I appreciate your insights, ma'am, but probably best if you head inside now."

She nodded as she shuffled back to her front door, mumbling. "Half my collectibles fell off the shelves while those fools was busy blowin' themselves up. Hmph."

Jogging across the street to where another group of spectators from down the block gathered, he gave them the same warning. "Shelter in place, and do what you can to avoid breathing in that stench. Give the firemen time to put out the flames and contain the chemicals."

They dispersed in a hurry when a new blaze broke out on the roof of the house next door to the main fire. Noah ran to the front door and banged on it. If the owners were inside, they might not realize their home was starting to burn in earnest. When no one answered, he went to the back of the house. There, a wooden shed crackled and sparked, already in flames. He couldn't let anyone inside die on his watch. He banged on the back door, then tried the knob. Again, no answer.

The fire truck sirens, faint a few minutes earlier, now blasted their arrival on Boxwood Lane. As Noah dashed to the front, he slapped at burning pieces of ash that floated down and singed his arms. He sought out Fire Chief Cummings while the men climbed off the trucks and unrolled hoses.

"It's a meth house, based on the odor. I managed to get all the neighbors to shelter in place inside their homes." Pointing to the adjacent homes, Noah said, "But the roof's burning on that blue house next door." Seized by a sudden coughing fit, he bent over, hands on knees. He straightened, still wheezing. "And a shed in the backyard is starting to flame. I banged on the doors but no response. There might be someone in there."

The chief nodded and signaled for two of his men to make entry and check for occupants. "If you know this is a meth house, why aren't you wearing your ventilator mask?"

At a loss for words, Noah froze, staring at Cummings. He'd screwed up. In his rush to make sure everyone else was okay, he hadn't put his own mask on.

"Well, don't just stand there, son," the chief said, raising his voice through his own ventilator. "Go get it, put it on. Then come back and set up a perimeter, okay?"

Giving him a thumbs-up, Noah sprinted toward his SUV, already getting short of breath. He opened the back and sorted through an equipment box. Blinking against the sting of chemicals, he wiped sweat from his forehead before pulling on the military-grade mask. He made sure it sealed tightly against his skin all the way around. It took him a minute to get used to viewing things through the plastic, but it was a heck of a lot better than going blind. Everyone in the sheriff's department had one and always carried it with them. But it would help if he just remembered to put it on *before* running into toxic fumes.

Grabbing a roll of barricade tape from the box, he headed back to the damaged properties. Though Noah didn't wish a fiery death on anyone, not even bad guys, his blood boiled with excitement. He wanted to be lead on this case. Wanted it so much, it burned in his gut like five-alarm chili. It was only fair—he'd been first on the scene. Besides, he was long overdue to be assigned an investigation to run. He hadn't been a rookie for a few years now, but between his penchant for joking around and being the youngest deputy, he was more often than not treated as one. This was the perfect case for him to show the department that he was more than just a funny guy. That they should be taking him seriously. Especially Sheriff Cassie Reed, his sister.

Speak of the devil. The sheriff's vehicle rolled down the street toward him, Cassie behind the wheel. Both the sheriff and her passenger already had their ventilators on. Noah approached the lowered passenger window, leaned down and looked into the crystal-blue eyes of a cute brunette with a mess of curls on her head. Granted, the mask hid most of her face, but even so…

She must be the new deputy from San Antonio. The

newbie looked past his mask-covered face, casing the scene like a well-honed professional. Impressed on all counts, Noah figured he just might have to reread the HR manual's section on dating coworkers.

"Got everything under control?" Cassie's ventilator muffled her voice.

He nodded. "I'm just about to cordon off the properties involved in the fire for Cummings. I'll meet up with you after you park."

Cassie nodded and continued down the street, followed by another SUV carrying his older brother, Chief Deputy Adam Reed, along with Deputies Sean Cavanaugh and Peter Grant. They must have left Dave Saunders in the office as the on-call deputy, which was fine with Noah. Dave had been a pain to work with since the day he was hired. Cassie thought she'd gotten Dave and his attitude straightened out last year. Cassie thought wrong.

Noah strung the barricade tape, then approached Cummings for an update. "Any sign of victims?"

"Not yet. Still too hot to get in there. But if we find any, they aren't going to be alive."

Scanning the street, Noah asked, "Will the people who live in the neighborhood be all right to stay here, or do they need to be evacuated?"

"They just need to stay inside until we get the fire out." Sweat ran down Cummings's face inside his mask. "We'll monitor the air quality, but they should be fine as long as they don't stand out here and breathe in fumes. If any of them have health conditions, they'll want to take extra measures to avoid inhaling this stuff." He

ran through some safety basics and gave Noah an estimation on when it might be safe to enter the building.

Noah gave him another thumbs-up and went off
to find Cassie. She stood across the street, talking to
Adam and the newbie. They huddled upwind of the
fumes, the other deputies in a group close by.

"…second one in less than four months," Cassie said
as he approached.

"In my experience, there's never just one or two."
Even with her respirator on, the newbie's confident tone
came through loud and clear. "Once we have a starting
point to investigate, I think we're going to find more
of them. Hopefully, in less-populated areas."

Cassie looked at Noah. "What have we got?"

"Everyone needs to avoid contact with these chemicals because they'll burn the skin. Hazmat suits are
recommended for anyone staying on the scene." Noah
took a deep breath of mask air, regretting the extra
onions he'd had on his breakfast sandwich. "No sign
of any victims yet. Chief Cummings estimates it may
be tomorrow before it's safe enough to send in the
hazmat team."

He widened his stance. He'd read somewhere that
power poses increased self-confidence.

"As to your point," he said, addressing the new deputy, "you're probably right. One of the residents on the
street said she'd heard rumors of meth houses popping
up in other parts of the county."

She gave him a slight nod but said nothing.

"Have you started interviewing neighbors yet?"
Cassie asked Noah.

Refusing to get defensive, he shook his head. "My main focus was on the safety of everyone in the immediate area. I'd planned to start knocking on doors once that was accomplished." No matter how well he performed on the job, Cassie always managed to find something that made him feel lacking.

Cassie turned to Adam. "Have Sean and Peter stay here with you to control the scene. If any of you go near the house, change into protective hazmat suits." She pointed for emphasis. "And keep your respirators on."

While Cassie issued orders, Noah took a moment to size up the new deputy. A few inches shorter than Cassie's five-nine, she appeared fit and capable. Fingernails short and unpolished. No rings; the only jewelry she wore was a pair of small stud earrings. Her white shirt was pressed, but he was pleased that her black jeans—the pants portion of the department's uniform—didn't hold ironed creases like Cassie's did. Resting her hands on her duty belt with an easy confidence, she kept her head on a constant swivel.

Seeing her next to Cassie, Noah couldn't help but notice the same authoritative ready-for-anything attitude. And he'd bet a six-pack of Lone Star longnecks that she was another by-the-booker, like his sister. That's about all he could tell about the newest member of their department, except for—beyond any doubt—she was definitely no rookie.

When Cassie's conversation with Adam ended, she approached Noah and the newbie. Between her directions to Adam and her somber expression now, he started to doubt her faith in him running this case. He took the bull by the horns.

"Can I speak with you?" Noah asked his sister.

"Wait here," she told the new deputy, then followed him several yards away to a patch of privacy. "What is it?"

"I was first on the scene. Established a perimeter, got the neighbors out of harm's way." Noah's respirator rattled as he inhaled a deep breath. "I want to take lead on this."

Cassie looked him square in the eye, and Noah's hope sank like a stone. Cassie had raised Adam, Noah and his twin brother, Nate, after their free-spirited mother disappeared without a word. He doubted she had an expression he couldn't identify the second it crossed her face, even while wearing a mask. Her brows drew together in a combination of sternness and sympathy. A look he resented.

"I'm tasking Adam with this case. I've got another assignment for you." She glanced over her shoulder, then met his eyes again. "I want you to partner with Deputy Delgado for a while. She knows law enforcement, has plenty of experience—but the way things are done in San Antonio may not be the way we do them around here. Show her the ropes. Get her used to dealing with the folks of Resolute, people who aren't just civilians we protect and serve but are also neighbors and friends."

Noah started to speak, but Cassie held up a finger to stop him.

"A couple of other things," she said. "This isn't some huge drug operation. Just an isolated incident or two of idiots who blew themselves up. So it's not really the big case you want."

"And the second thing?" Noah pressed his lips into a thin line, determined to remain professional.

"I arrived here in time to see you at your car. You didn't follow protocol, Noah." Cassie's voice held an officious tone. "I know you were hurrying to take care of other people, but in a situation like this, you *have* to put your mask on first. You were doing the wrong thing for the right reason, and I get that. But until you're able to stick to protocol, follow the rules, do the right thing no matter the reason—you won't be ready to take lead on an investigation."

During his years with the department, Noah had never been angry with Cassie or envious of his older brother. Now he was both. Angry with Cassie for not believing in him. Envious of Adam for being more respected within the department. These unfamiliar emotions made him disappointed in himself. And the only person who could fix the situation was Noah himself. So he sucked it up and followed his boss back to where the newbie stood, now holding something furry.

"What have you got here?" Noah reached out and pet the rabbit.

"Poor little bunny came hopping over this way from the fire. He looks a little singed and a lot scared."

"Noah, this is Deputy Brianna Delgado. Brianna, Deputy Noah Reed."

Standing in a circle of masked faces, Noah couldn't help himself. He breathed in and out with as much noise as possible. "Brianna, I am your father," he said, mimicking Darth Vader.

"Be serious, Noah," Cassie admonished, no doubt wincing inside her mask.

Probably not the best time or place for a joke, he conceded, but the sharpness of his disappointment had apparently dulled his better judgment. Besides, who didn't love *Star Wars*?

To her credit, the newbie ignored his inanity and stretched out her hand. "Call me Bree." She looked at Cassie. "You, too, Sheriff."

Cassie nodded. "Bree, it is. I'd like you to ride with Noah this week, maybe longer. He'll help get you familiar with the town and the way we do things in Resolute. I'm sure San Antonio operated at a much more hectic pace."

"An all-hands-on-deck for a meth-house explosion first thing in the morning is pretty hectic even in San Antonio. Sure didn't expect this type of excitement here." Bree glanced down at the bunny. "What about my orientation meeting?"

"We can finish that later. You two go ahead, get out of here. Swing by the office first. Helen has your badge and ID, Bree." Cassie's gaze focused on Noah. "Respond to any calls. During down times, show her around town."

"You got it, Sheriff." As frustrated as Noah was, he kept it from his tone. Last thing he wanted was for

Bree to wonder why he hadn't been named as officer in charge at the scene. But his use of Cassie's title would let his sister know that he was definitely miffed.

He caught Bree's eye and motioned for her to follow him.

"I'll find the owner quickly." She held up the rabbit.

"There's no telling how long that would take. We'll drop it off at our animal shelter." He started for his vehicle, looking back over his shoulder on the way.

She'd crossed a lawn and was knocking on the front door of a house. When it opened, she showed the occupants the rabbit; they shook their heads, then pointed to a house two doors down.

Noah watched as Bree went to the indicated house. The door opened, a little girl squealed and took the animal, hugging it and burying her face in its fur. Nodding, Bree backed away, then turned and jogged toward him.

As annoyed as he was, the sight of the curvy deputy sporting such a serious frown coaxed a smile from him. She better figure out how to relax, or she'd have a hard time fitting in around here.

"Told you I'd find his owner in a matter of minutes."

He laughed at the satisfaction in her voice. "You got lucky. Probably 'cause you had four rabbit's feet."

As she groaned, he started toward his vehicle again. "Pick up the pace."

All right, then. He hadn't gotten the case and was stuck driving the newbie around. So what? Could be worse. A lot worse. Eventually, his break would come.

For now, he'd bide his time, spend the day—no, make that a week or longer—with the cute deputy from San Antonio, who seemed competent, if a little stiff. Well, if anyone could get her to loosen up, it'd be him.

He always could turn a loss into a win.

SOME DAYS, she just couldn't win for losing.

Bree speed-walked to keep up with Noah's long stride as they headed to his vehicle. Aggravating man. His mask made it impossible to tell, but she'd bet her first paycheck he wore a smug grin that she'd love to knock off his face. A drop-dead gorgeous face, from what she saw of it before he'd gotten his mask on. But that wouldn't stop her from walloping him if he got out of line.

Noah Reed was nothing like his sister. Clearly younger than the sheriff, he seemed eager and passionate. Which she liked, but he was also irreverent in an annoying way. Which she didn't. Thank goodness they weren't being partnered longtime. She'd only be stuck with him for a week, maybe less if she could prove herself. After that she'd be glad to be on her own, where no one would be tempted to get up in her business.

She had her reasons for taking this job, for moving to a small town in a small county. Reasons she wasn't prepared to share with anyone. And partners tended to be nosy. *Well, Deputy Reed, you're going to learn real fast that being a loner doesn't mean I'm not a damn good cop.* Interview witnesses, review evidence, track down bad guys—classic policing.

She certainly didn't need some dewy-faced deputy

babysitting her, even if he happened to be hot. But so what if he *was* hot? She'd been trained to be observant. Didn't mean she wanted to get involved with him—or anyone else, for that matter. She had enough issues in her life to handle without becoming entangled in someone else's.

Stay frosty.

Once inside the patrol vehicle, doors firmly closed, Bree removed her respirator mask, fastened her seat belt and focused straight ahead. When Noah didn't start the car, she glanced over and found him giving her an easy smile.

"Care to share the joke, or do you plan to sit there all day?"

"There's really no joke. I'd guessed at what you would look like without your mask, and I was wrong." His grin deepened on one side.

Bree lifted her left arm and looked at her watch. "Wow, not even two hours on the job. Gee, Deputy Reed, I think you broke the record for the fastest on-the-job flirting in my career."

His smile disappeared as if it had never been there. "Hey, that's not what I meant. It's like when you hear someone on the radio and imagine what they look like based on their voice. And then you see their face, and it's not what you pictured in your head. I—never mind." Resting his left wrist on the steering wheel, he turned over the engine and put the car into gear and edged around the emergency vehicles.

Running his words through her mind again, Bree acknowledged to herself that she might have overreacted to his comment. In an attempt to restore some equilibrium, she asked, "Where are we off to first? Pretty sure nothing in town can beat this excitement." She waved her hand to indicate the first responders still swarming the street.

"Oh, you'd be surprised. And that's why I'm here to show you the ropes. We have plenty of excitement in good old Resolute. Why, just last week someone let dozens of chickens loose in the city hall during a meeting about repaving the roads." A dimple popped in his right cheek. "Headline the next morning was 'Council Meeting: Nothing but Tar and Feathers.'"

She turned away and smirked to herself. She refused to encourage Noah's odd sense of humor.

"You'd be wrong to think this town has nothing much going on." He glanced away from the road and caught her eye. "Resolute has a way of keeping you on your toes. But not to worry. After a week riding with me, you'll have a good start on learning all of Boone County's dirty little secrets."

Secrets.

Bree looked out her side window, the glass reflecting a deep V between her brows. *This is not what I signed up for.* By resigning from the San Antonio PD and accepting the job in Boone County, she thought she'd traded being on her toes for being a flatfoot. Traded the action of big-city law enforcement for walking a beat in a sleepy little town in South Central Texas. A price she'd willingly pay to keep her badge.

Secrets. She hated them. They had a nasty way of

biding their time, then rearing their ugly faces when you least expected them.

She could do without learning Boone County's secrets. She had her own to worry about.

Chapter Two

It was turning into a banner first day. After she and Noah stopped by the justice building to pick up her badge, they were dispatched to the local high school, where a break-in over the weekend had been reported. So much for a slow-paced small-town crime rate.

The downtown shops and businesses of Resolute passed by Bree's window as Noah drove through town. Well-maintained historic homes gave way to shotgun houses on small lots, and as they approached Resolute High, Bree craned her neck to take it all in. "This is a much bigger school than I imagined."

"They built the new additions about five years ago, after they were finally able to buy the surrounding land for the sports fields." Noah's lips twisted to the side. "Would've been nice to have this when I went here."

"Are all the fields just for this one school?"

"Gosh, no. It's a sports complex for the area. Kids who live in the county, or in even smaller towns with no schools, are bused in for classes." Noah parked in front of the main building. "And the fields are used by other schools in the county that don't have facilities to host home games."

As they walked toward the front of the building, Bree checked out the school's entrance, searching for vulnerabilities in Resolute High's security system. A surveillance camera, aimed at the front doors. *Sweet.* That camera would have caught the thieves if they entered this way.

Noah pushed through the front doors and held them open for her.

Unfortunately, no signs of forced entry indicated these doors weren't the thieves' point of entry. Bree checked her watch: quarter past ten in the morning. Except for those with free periods, most of the kids would be in class. She didn't need to speed walk to keep up with Noah. He meandered down the nearly empty main hallway. Maybe taking a walk down memory lane, since he was checking out the glass display cases hanging on the walls. What was he looking at?

Each one contained sports trophies and pictures of the school's star athletes for a given year. He paused at one, and Bree moved closer to read the names. The only player featured for that year was Nathan Reed.

"Relative of yours?" Bree tapped on the glass.

"My twin."

Her eyes narrowed as she looked at Noah, then the pictures in the display case and back to Noah. "You two don't look anything alike."

"Keen observation, Deputy." His mouth pulled into a smirk. "Sure you're not a detective?"

"Hilarious. It's an interrogation method, wise guy. Stating the obvious. Gets suspects to talk."

"So I'm a suspect and my crime is not looking like my twin?" Noah leaned in as if conspiring with her. "We're fraternal, by the way—not identical. But don't tell anyone. Most of the town can't tell us apart." He took a few steps down the hall, then turned back when she didn't follow him. "Come on, newbie. The principal is waiting for us."

But she wasn't done looking at the display case. "Impressive. Football quarterback, baseball pitcher, captain of the basketball team." Bree again glanced at Noah, automatically trying to peel back the layers of this man she'd be working with for the next week. What kind of man was he? Someone she could count on or just another class clown? "Weren't you into sports?"

"I was."

"Then why isn't your picture in there?" Was it her imagination, or did his posture stiffen?

"Only star players for each year are featured, and Nate was the MVP of every sport when we were seniors." The line of his jaw tightened. "If you squint, you can see me just there." He tapped his index finger against the glass case. "In the team pictures with everyone else."

She bent forward until her nose practically touched the glass and peered inside the case. Yep, there he was.

"Come on. Principal's expecting us."

Bree followed, almost growling when his pace once more went into hyperdrive. On purpose? She wouldn't put it past him. Aggravating man. "So your twin—

your *fraternal* twin, Nathan—is he also a deputy?" It seemed like half the sheriff's department consisted of Reeds.

"Only one of the four of us who didn't go into law enforcement." Noah stopped at a door marked Principal and knocked.

"Come in," a deep voice bellowed from behind the door, and Noah opened it. "Ah, good, good. You're here." A paunchy older man with a bad comb-over came out from behind his desk and shook their hands. "Seems like a dog's age since I've seen you, Noah."

"I've found it's harder to get sent to the principal's office once you graduate." Noah smirked, then motioned toward Bree. "Mr. Jackson, this is Deputy Brianna Delgado. Today's her first day on the job, but she comes with a lot of experience from the San Antonio PD."

"That so?" Jackson gave her an appraising look, nodded his apparent approval and returned to his chair. "Nice to meet you, Deputy."

"Pleasure is mine, Mr. Jackson." Should've known the principal and Noah would be well acquainted. Everyone in this town probably knew everyone else. Bree assumed an impassive expression as she and Noah took the two visitor chairs. She pulled her notepad and pen from her shirt pocket, ready to question Jackson.

"Been to any of our basketball games this year?" The principal looked at Noah. "Heck of a season so far."

"I've been to a few. Team's looking good." Noah leaned forward in his chair, arms on his knees. "But I made it to every football game. What do you think Armentrout's chances are to get recruited by University of Texas?"

Jackson waved his hand. "He's a shoo-in for the Longhorns. But I know for a fact Texas A&M wants him, and I've heard rumors Baylor will be throwing their hat in the ring."

"Kid's got a bright future, that's for sure." Noah glanced at Bree. When she arched one brow in his direction, he pulled out his own notepad and cleared his throat. "So, Mr. Jackson, what can you tell us about this break-in?"

"All I know is they hit the science, computer and athletic departments. I told the department heads to cobble together lists of whatever they found missing or damaged."

Bree kept her pen poised over her pad. "Mr. Jackson, we'll need to see the footage from your security cameras."

Jackson gave a sardonic laugh. "Which cameras?"

"All of them. I noticed one by the front entrance when we came in, but there were no signs of forced entry." Bree tapped her pen on the paper. "I'm assuming the perps entered another way, so we'll need footage from all exterior doors."

"Oh, we know exactly where they got in. Through the gymnasium door. Tried to pry it open, then broke the glass right out of it."

"Wasn't your alarm company alerted?"

The principal offered a pleasant smile. "Most incidents these days are nothing more than harmless pranks, like what you might expect seniors to get up to right before graduation." He shot Noah a knowing look. "You can find out more about those from this guy here. True, he never broke in—but as I recall, he masterminded most of the pranks during his years here at Resolute High."

"Why, Mr. Jackson, that is so not true," Noah's overly dramatic protest almost made her laugh. "You're making me look bad in front of Deputy Delgado."

That piqued her interest. But stories to ask him about another day. She turned to face the principal again. "May I ask what point you're making, sir? About the pranks?"

Jackson stood, apparently ready to shoo them away.

Noah got to his feet, but Bree remained sitting. She'd obviously hit a nerve, and she wasn't letting Mr. Jackson off the hook that easily. Keeping kids safe was a big deal to her, and it should be to this man, too.

Jackson must have realized she wasn't ready to leave, because he plopped back into his chair. "We had some budget cuts about four, five years back and decided we could save money by getting rid of the monitored alarm system. Like I said, we typically only have pranks."

Budget cuts that happened right when the athletic fields were purchased. Bree clenched her teeth and her jaw went rigid. *Figures.* She breathed in deeply, nostrils flaring as she struggled to regain her impartiality. But based on the principal's reaction, she failed miserably. Damn her lack of a poker face.

The middle-aged principal sat up straighter, his face coloring red. "It's the school board that makes those kinds of decisions, Deputy, and I make do with what I get. A situation I'm sure is quite similar to your department being at the mercy of Boone County's budget."

His point might be valid, but the decision to save money by sacrificing security wasn't. "We still need the footage from the cameras."

Jackson shrugged. "A while back we had some technical problems with them recording. It's been on our list of things to take care of."

"May I ask how long a while? A couple days? Weeks?"

"I'd say more like a couple years. We've just never had a serious need for them."

"I know. You've only had pranks." She stood. "Thank you for your time, Mr. Jackson." Then to Noah: "Let's go talk to the heads of the departments that were hit." She left the office and walked down the hallway.

After a moment, footsteps followed her. "Hold on, Bree."

She kept walking.

"Delgado, wait."

She stopped and faced Noah.

"Is there something wrong?"

"You tell me." Bree glared at him. "Your school board thinks it's more important to build out the athletic department and fields than to provide security for the school itself, as well as the students." She bet he regretted telling her about the school expansion now.

"Come on. This is Texas. You know—Friday-night football, barbecue, Lone Star Beer." When Bree didn't return his grin, Noah asked, "You *were* born in Texas, weren't you?"

"I was, and I'm for all the Texas traditions." She inhaled a deep breath, then exhaled, accompanied by an internal chant of *You wanted a small town, you got a small town*.

"Look, this is a small county, and the school district doesn't have a budget the size of those in places like San Antonio. Everyone's doing the best they can." Bree opened her mouth, but Noah held up a finger. "And that's another thing that's different from San Antonio, where most people you deal with are strangers. Here, these people are our friends and neighbors. Sometimes for generations. Law enforcement in Resolute is true community policing."

Bree huffed a breath of frustration. "The bottom line is, one of your so-called 'friends' or 'neighbors' now knows how to break into this school. If the principal—no, make that the school board—doesn't stop prioritizing sports over safety and invest in an adequate surveillance system, statistics say the thieves will come back. And frankly, I think your principal back there has more power in this regard than he lets on."

"That man in there—" Noah pointed back toward the office they'd just left "—has been the principal of this school for more than two decades. He's always been trapped within the confines of the school board's budget and always had to rob Peter to pay Paul. I agree, he needs to find money somewhere and reallocate it to school security. But let's give him the benefit of the doubt for now. Maybe he's hit a brick wall with the finances, and the board needs to answer to that."

Bree opened her mouth, a retort on the tip of her

tongue. Then she snapped her mouth shut and walked off in the direction she'd been heading. There was no point arguing with someone as stubborn as Noah Reed. Especially since he had some valid points. And some of hers were best kept to herself.

"Where are you going?" he called after her.

"Science department." She picked up her pace. Let him catch up to her for once.

"See you there."

Bree slid to a stop and looked behind her at Noah's retreating back. "Why are you going that way?"

He turned his head around. "'Cause the science department is this way." He and his annoying smug grin made a right turn down another hallway and disappeared.

Muttering a curse, Bree made a U-turn and followed him. *Such* an aggravating man.

NOAH SCOWLED AT the pile of swept-up glass in a corner of the chemistry lab. Wanton vandalism stuck in his craw. A darn shame to waste resources like that.

"As you can see, they broke a lot of glassware." Joan Metcalf, the fortysomething head of the science department, was a barrel-bodied woman with an ample bosom, rosy cheeks and a dimpled grin. This morning, though, her grin was absent as she picked up a jagged shard of glass from the counter and dropped it into a nearby trash can. "But what's on the floor doesn't begin to account for all that's missing. I've asked Mr. Jennings, the chemistry teacher—this is his classroom—to provide me with a complete inventory of the missing items. Should be ready in no time. He's extremely organized."

Noah stepped around shattered beakers and funnels. "Do you have a preliminary idea of what's missing?"

"Well, now, that's the strange thing. Looks like they took a bit of everything. Bunsen burners, mortars and pestles. There's really no rhyme or reason to what was stolen." The department head shrugged. "The biology lab is the same. Dissecting-tool kits, petri dishes, litmus papers... It makes no sense."

"Will the biology teacher also do up an inventory list?" Bree asked.

"Has to. For the insurance claim." Metcalf's brow furrowed. "The physics teacher, too. Neither of their labs have as much damage. Even so, we moved all classes to other rooms so you can dust for fingerprints and whatever else you need to do for your investigation."

Bree glanced around the room, and Noah could see the exact direction of her thoughts. *Don't say it. Don't say it.* "How many classes per day are in each of the science labs, and how many students per class?"

Noah inhaled. *She said it.* Tactful, Bree was not.

"Well, we have..." Joan faltered. "I see what you're getting at, Deputy Delgado. Fingerprints *would* be a challenge."

"Not a challenge. An impossibility."

"But you did the right thing. I only wish more people thought about possible evidence being destroyed." Noah smiled at Joan. "And, of course, it will keep the students from getting cut."

Joan returned his smile. "Thank you. This is the

first time since I've been here that anything like this has happened. It's a bit jarring."

"Yes, it can be, and I'm sorry you have to deal with this. Let me ask you, have—"

"Have you or the other teachers had problems with any of the sutdents?" Bree interrupted. "You know, someone who might have wanted to get even for a bad grade or recent discipline?"

"Not that I'm aware of." Joan's vacant gaze drifted toward the ceiling as she seemed to sort through memories. "I know there are students who act up in class or smart-mouth the teachers, but as a department, we try to handle it with humor rather than escalate the situation. Nothing stands out as having warranted this kind of destruction."

"Thank you for your time, and we'd appreciate copies of those lists." Noah handed her one of his cards. "You can email the inventories to the address on there."

Nodding, Joan took the card. "Stay as long you like. As I said, no students will be using this room. But I must get ready for my next class. You know where to go from here?"

"Yes, ma'am, and thank you."

"Please call us if you or the other teachers think of anything that might help." Bree gave her a distracted smile.

Once Joan left, Noah and Bree went into investigative mode. As if they'd been partners for years, they seemed in tune with one another as they worked the room, making notes and taking cell phone pictures of the damage, all the while looking for the smallest shred of evidence that might prove useful.

Finally, Noah closed his notebook and tucked away his cell phone. "Next up, biology lab."

Without a word, Bree returned to the main hall. *Where she'll have to wait for my directions.*

Noah shook his head as she strode away, her gun riding low on her hip. *Oh, man. You're in so much trouble with this one.*

He followed her, forcing his thoughts away from the fascinating view ahead of him. The week couldn't be over fast enough.

Chapter Three

After speaking with the biology and physics teachers, taking more notes and pictures of the damage in their classrooms, Noah led Bree through the maze of hallways to the computer lab.

Back in the day, Ben Irving, now head of the computer science department, had been a classmate of Noah's. A friendly guy, Ben had always entertained with hilarious jokes and stories. At five foot nine and well over two hundred pounds, with eyes that twinkled and a ready smile, he was hard not to like.

"Ben. How's it going?" Noah glanced around the vandalized room. "Other than the obvious."

"Could've been worse." Ben shrugged. "I heard about that explosion. Right in the middle of Rosemont, right? What a crazy world we live in."

"Tell me about it." Noah grimaced. After a moment of considering that crazy world, he managed a smile. "Ben, this is Brianna Delgado, our newest deputy. Bree, Ben Irving. Champion gamer and nerd extraordinaire."

Ben laughed. "Not much time these days for video

games, not with a new baby in the house. But you know how it is—once a nerd, always a nerd."

"Nice to meet you, Ben. I happen to have a special fondness for nerds." Bree smiled, and Noah almost gasped. Those upturned lips radiated a genuine warmth that lit up her whole stunning face. "I used to pretty much be one myself."

"Unlike your partner here—" he clapped Noah on the shoulder "—who was forever making fun of my nerd status. But I won't waste your time churning up old stories about what a jerk he was. Here, let me show you what the thieves got up to." Ben pointed to evidence that the burglars had tried to steal some of the laptops. "They probably gave up because of the cable locks we use."

Bree examined one of the locks up close, then got on her knees to look at the underside of the table.

"Those are mighty thin cables." Noah ran his fingers along one of the metal cords. "Seems like they could have just cut it with something."

"It's carbon steel," Ben said. "They'd need bolt cutters to make a dent."

"It also has an anti-shear sleeve around it. Makes it hard for cutters to grab onto the cable." Bree, still kneeling by the table, waved Noah over. "Look underneath. Instead of just looping the cable around the table leg, they've got a round bar soldered to both ends of the table frame."

Noah got down on his knees to examine the setup, distracted by Bree's nearness. Her scent—cool and refreshing, like the air after an early-spring storm—aroused his appetite to taste her, head to toe. *Get a grip, man.*

Ben beamed. "I came up with that idea, and some of the kids from shop class welded the bars to the tables for extra credit."

"Brilliant idea." Bree smiled again, and a ping of annoyance shot through Noah. She had not once favored him with such a smile. But her excitement over the security measure was palatable and contagious. "See, Noah, if they were just wound around the legs, all someone had to do was set the computer on the floor, lift the table and slide the cable off. But with them looped around the bar that's attached, they'd have to take the whole table with them."

"You ought to patent that." Noah stood and reached out a hand to help Bree to her feet, but she rose on her own. Figured.

"Did anyone steal a computer?" Bree asked. "Before the bars were added?"

Ben twisted his mouth to the side and looked away.

"This will be kept confidential, if that's what you're worried about." Noah glanced at Bree, who nodded in agreement.

"Well, yes. Once. That's why I added the bars. A couple of years ago, a student took one of the laptops in exactly the manner you described." Ben gave them a sheepish smile. "When I started teaching here, it amazed me that the administration didn't seem to realize how easy it was to steal a computer. I spoke to Principal Jackson about it, but he said they had no budget. And since there hadn't been any thefts up until that point, he couldn't justify the expense." He looked down at the floor and scoffed. "Okay, so I get it. Kids need textbooks. Teachers need supplies. Money only goes so far. So I took matters into my own hands."

Bree's million-dollar smile morphed from genuine to cynical. "So the theft went unreported?"

Man, she is a tough nut.

If Ben noticed, he didn't seem troubled by her implication. "I couldn't do it. I figured out who had taken it almost immediately. When I confronted the kid, he copped to it right away. Told me he had a part-time job evenings and weekends, and he'd fallen behind in school. His family couldn't afford to buy a computer, so he *borrowed* it."

Now Noah was curious. "Did he return it?"

"Eventually. I let him *borrow* it for a few more days while I refurbished an old one that was gathering dust in our supply closet. When I got it up and running, I signed it out to him for the rest of the year. After that, he stayed on top of his coursework despite having the job. Graduated with honors and earned a full ride to Texas State. Before leaving for San Marcos, he wrote me a note and gave me credit for his success. Man, I've got to tell you—days like that make teaching worthwhile. I still have the note."

Noah watched the judgment on Bree's face soften. *So you're not all stone and thorns, are you?* He turned to Ben. "We'll need a few more minutes to look over the area and take some pictures, then we'll be out of your hair."

"Take your time. I'm off to serve time as study hall supervisor."

Noah shook hands with Ben and gave him a card. "If you do find anything missing or damaged, give us a call. And we need to get together one of these days. It's been ages."

"I hope you're serious, because Mary and the kids would love to see you."

"I am."

"Great. I'll have her text you to work out the day and time. And of course, Deputy Delgado, you should join us, too."

"Um, thank you, but—"

Ben held up a forestalling hand. "Save your protests. You'd be doing me a favor. If my wife found out someone new to town wasn't included, she'd have my hide. So I and my hide are not taking no for an answer. Bring your husband or significant other as well. Heck, bring your dog, if you have one. We're all about family-style dining at mi casa. It'll be loud and rambunctious, but you won't find a better cook than my Mary." He patted his paunch affectionately.

Noah watched her waffle. "Oh, come on. I promise to be on my best behavior." He cocked his head, widened his eyes and blinked enticingly.

And, wonder of wonders, he coaxed one of those dazzling smiles from her.

"Your best behavior, eh?" Bree scoffed. "It'll be nice to finally see that."

Ben burst out laughing, and Bree turned her smile his way. "Thanks, I'd love to come. It'll just be me, though.

No significant other, no dog. And only if you call me Bree."

Noah hadn't had time to consider her personal situation before now, but he was a little too glad that she wasn't involved with anyone.

"Done!" Ben exclaimed. "Mary will be the envy of town at being the first to host the new deputy. You've done me a solid, Bree. Now then, let me get your cell number so my wife can text you the details."

Noah had joined Ben and Mary for dinner on numerous occasions, but he couldn't remember ever looking forward to it as much as this time. And he wasn't ashamed to admit, if only to himself, that Bree was the reason.

As Bree and Ben went about exchanging phone numbers, he walked around the computer lab, taking pictures of the minimal damage and fighting a Cheshire cat grin. Every little bit he learned about Bree made him hunger to find out more.

Cell numbers exchanged, Ben left them to finish searching the classroom for clues that might point to the thieves' identities. Noah finally glanced at Bree. "Four down and one to go. Ready to head to the athletic department?"

"Lead on."

As they traversed the building's corridors, Noah glanced at her. "You know, you really won over Ben. And in Resolute, that's a surefire path to good policing."

Her forehead creased, and not in a good way. "Good policing is accomplished through sharp observation, solid reporting and thorough follow-up. In no manual that I've ever read does it say anything about the warm-and-fuzzies."

Seriously? Why couldn't women just accept compliments? He'd never understood it. Cassie was that way, too. It made no sense to him. "Then you haven't read the right manuals."

She looked at him, wild-eyed. "What are you talking about?"

"Just, you know, you seemed to get along better with Ben than with Principal Jackson."

Bree stopped in her tracks. "The difference is that Ben found a way to fix a problem, despite the school's refusal to pay for it. *And* he managed to help a student in need. Whereas the principal just waved away security issues and blamed it on the county."

Noah grudgingly admitted to himself that Bree had a point. A tight budget *was* a sorry excuse for sacrificing security in a school. He made a mental note to check with the rest of the county schools, make sure they weren't in the same position.

They continued to the gym in silence.

"Let me do the talking with this next guy," Noah told her in no uncertain terms.

Bree's tone turned icy. "And why is that, exactly?"

"Because you won't be able to keep your face from showing how you feel about money being spent on sports. Trust me. It would be best if Coach doesn't see that."

"I have no problem with money being spent on

sports, unless there's a more important need for it elsewhere."

"Which there always is," Noah countered.

Bree grabbed his arm to slow his furious pace. "Exactly. Not that it ever matters. But you never answered me—the coach not knowing my opinion would be best for who?"

If ever there was a divide between big-city versus small-town policing, here it was. Plain as the nose on Bree's face. She was just too nearsighted to see it. "It would be best for our investigation. And best for you, if you must know."

"So all this concern of yours is really just for me?" She tapped her chest as she stared at him.

Noah glared. Stubborn, obstinate woman. She wasn't going to let this drop, so fine. She wanted brutal honesty? She'd get it. "Look, our department has a darn-good working relationship with the people of Resolute, and we'd like to keep it that way. Since you're new, you're making a first impression on everyone you meet. If you start ragging on Coach Crawford about how his equipment might not have been stolen if the school had spent more money on security, you will *not* be making a good first impression."

Bree tsked. "I had no plans to rag on anyone, let alone your exalted coach. But let me remind you, he's not a god. He's just one person."

Noah wanted to shake her. "One person who has absolutely nothing to do with the school's budget or how it's allocated. So save your holier-than-thou condemnation. What's even more important for you to under-

stand is that every person who has gone to Resolute
High for the past twenty years knows Coach Crawford.
The kids love him. The parents love him. And yes, the
school board loves him. Why? Because he's not only
the basketball coach—he's the director of the entire
athletics department. He's responsible for hiring every
other coach and assistant coach they have. The buck
stops with him, and he wins games. Lots and lots of
games. Football, baseball, basketball. You name it, he
wins it. Year after year. So trust me when I say that if
you tick him off, which you most certainly will with
that sour expression on your face, word will spread like
lightning. And any chance you have of making friends
or succeeding in any kind of meaningful investigation
will be harder than finding a black cat in a coal cellar."

It wasn't like him to just lay it out there like that,
especially this soon after meeting someone. But if she
wanted to last as a deputy in Resolute, she needed to
understand the lay of the land. Seemed simple enough
to him, but he should have expected her not to take his
advice lying down.

"You don't understand what it's like to be a woman
in law enforcement."

He rolled his eyes. "Please. I have a sister who's the
town sheriff. I beg to disagree."

"In a small town," Bree snapped. "Where half the
force is related to her. Not the same thing at all, and
don't even bother trying to argue that it is. For most
women who carry guns… Well, let me put it this way.
I'm used to not making friends. And the few I had

didn't last long. So now I just get the job done, as professionally as possible, and call it a day."

"Have you considered balancing your cold aloofness and heated judgment with a little cordiality?"

She clenched her teeth, the muscles in her jaw flexing. "It's been my experience, Deputy Reed, that at the end of the day, people care more about me getting their stolen belongings back or locking up the perp who assaulted them than they do about me being Suzy Sunshine." A shadow of sorrow slid across her face before her features once again hardened.

Without warning, Noah's anger deflated. What had happened to her that made her so harsh? Did he really want to know? Seemed like she had some serious emotional baggage, and that spelled *messy* any way you looked at it. He had his own fish to fry. Why complicate his life?

His gaze lingered on Bree's face, and he knew the answer. Behind her words, behind her fleeting look of melancholy, there was a story. *I want to know that story.* More than anything, he longed to see that smile of hers again. That beautiful, genuine, soul-lifting smile. No matter what it cost.

"Maybe you've just been working in the wrong town." He held open the door that led to the gym. "But I'm still doing the talking."

COACH CRAWFORD'S OFFICE fit Bree's expectations, for the most part. Utilitarian, as everything was in a school, but large and well furnished. A small trophy case on one wall and a mini-fridge next to a couch.

Ben Irving was protecting expensive laptops by utilizing shop-class kids, while the athletic department swam in luxuries.

A disapproving scowl tugged at her face, and she made a concerted effort to pull it back to at least a neutral expression. Noah had been right to call her out on that, but it didn't mean she had to like it.

Pasting a smile on her face, she shook Crawford's outstretched hand when Noah made the introductions.

"Nice to meet you, Deputy Delgado." He nodded once to her, then turned a smiling face toward Noah. "And boy, is it good to see you. Resolute High sure got boring after you graduated." Crawford's eyes shifted back to Bree. "You should have seen this guy in school. No matter how bad a day it was, he could cheer everyone up with a joke. He could even break up fights between players on the field with his sense of humor."

Trying to fit in, Bree laughed. But when she glanced at Noah, he seemed more annoyed than affable. A minute ago, he was all but worshipping the coach. What had changed? He hadn't reacted this way when Ben brought up the good old days. Even the principal's comments hadn't bothered him. But almost the first thing all three men had referred to was Noah's jokes. Maybe he was getting tired of being called a jokester.

Noah cleared his throat. "I hear your department got hit during the break-in."

"Yeah, they broke in through the main doors to the gymnasium. Really made a mess."

"Do you have a list of the stolen items?" Bree's pad

was already in her hand. "And has anyone been inside the athletics building today other than you?"

"I made an announcement this morning that all classes would be held outside today, so no one other than me has been inside. And I do have a list, but it's a weird one." The coach picked up a paper from his desk. "A few bats, some baseballs and footballs, one tennis racket. Who steals just one racket?" The coach handed her the handwritten list. "Nothing that we can't replace. But since they came in through our door, I figured I'd better report my losses, too."

"What do you mean when you say the stolen items are nothing you can't replace?" Bree asked him. Noah side-eyed her with a warning, but she ignored him.

"They didn't take that much stuff. Hardly a drop in the annual budget for my department."

Drop in the bucket. Annual budget. Bree tried. She clamped her mouth shut. She even rolled her lips in between her teeth. But heaven help her, a sharp retort fought its way to the tip of her tongue, ready to fly.

Noah must have sensed what was about to happen, because he spoke up just in time. "Did you do a thorough inventory of the entire building?" He even shifted his position, completely avoiding her laser-like glare.

The coach nodded. "Checked everything."

Bree hooked her thumbs on her duty belt in a challenging stance. "We'll just do a quick walk-through, see if we notice anything else amiss."

"Help yourselves. If you have any questions, I'll be here for another half hour. Then I have a class."

Before leaving, Bree asked, "Will we need keys to open any doors?"

"Unfortunately, no. They cut every padlock off. Even from the rooms they didn't steal anything from."

With a sharp nod, Bree left the office but paused just outside the door.

"Nice seeing you, Noah." Coach chuckled. "And good luck with your new partner. What was your sister thinking, pairing up Deputy All Business with Deputy Nothing but Fun?"

Noah gave a half-hearted laugh, then joined Bree.

To avoid another argument about sports versus security, she asked, "Do you have particular areas you want to check out?"

"I wonder if there are less-trafficked ones, where we might be able to pull some prints." Noah led the way to a room off a side hall. "This is the laundry room. Coach was in charge of washing all the team uniforms. Said he learned how during his brief stint in the NFL, and apparently there's an art to not destroying them. There might be a baseball or basketball coach who helps, but no one else has ever been allowed in here."

The room held a few huge washing machines and one dryer. An industrial floor polisher sat in one corner.

"Why aren't there more dryers?" Bree asked.

"Uniforms are always hung to dry. Only towels and socks go in the dryer." Noah pointed to a wall of swing-out drying racks.

Bree opened a cabinet door near the sink. "Nothing

but OxiClean, a couple different brands of laundry detergent and some general cleaning supplies."

Noah peered into the storage space, closed the cabinet and moved to another; this one full of clean, folded towels. "I can't imagine anyone breaking into the school to steal stuff and wasting time in here."

Bree nodded in agreement. "Less traffic but nothing worth stealing."

They moved on to the equipment rooms. Each consisted of a sturdy chain-link cage contained within three sides of drywall. The doors, also of metal chain link, were set in the fourth walls of the cages, and the padlocks that had provided security lay on the ground, their shanks cleanly cut.

Noah crouched next to one and, without touching, eyed it more closely. "I'll ask Coach to make sure everyone continues to stay out until we can get someone here to take prints."

"Let's check out the point of entry." Bree turned in a circle. "Where's the gymnasium's front door?"

Noah led her along a side hallway to the front entrance of the building. "This is where people enter and exit for basketball games."

The doorframe itself was damaged near the handle, where the thief had apparently tried to pry it open before resorting to breaking the glass.

"There's not enough glass broken out for a man to go *through* the opening." Noah squatted to examine the broken glass piled up against the base of the door. "They just broke out enough to reach through, unlock the door and waltz on in."

Bree stepped back several feet to take in the overall picture. "That wouldn't have worked."

Noah swiveled around in his crouch, his face screwed up in a questioning glance. "What are you talking about?"

"They could reach in and turn the bolt lock near the handle, but there's another lock at the bottom of the door that can only be unlocked with a key."

Taking a pen from his pocket, Noah moved a piece of glass, revealing the bottom lock. "Son of a gun. Whoever did this had to have access to a key."

Bree nodded. "It had to be an inside job." She considered different scenarios. "If they broke the glass, unlocked the bottom lock and came in, the door would have pushed the glass away. So the thief unlocked the door from the inside, left through it with the stolen property and *then* broke the glass from the outside. Trying to make it look like a break-in."

Noah seemed to process what she said. "You're right. They were just too dumb to think out their whole plan. If they'd just opened the door to push back the broken glass..."

"We still would have noticed the bottom lock."

"*You* still would have noticed it. I didn't even think about it." Noah stood and shoved his hands in his pockets. "Good catch, Delgado."

She shrugged. "I'm just surprised this is the point of entry. With all the money thrown at this department, I'd have thought the gym would be harder to get into than a virgin on her wedding night."

Noah snorted. "Why, Deputy Delgado. I'm surprised by your turn of phrase."

Her mouth kicked up at the corners. "Just been trying to make a good first impression. Now that I'm past that stage with you, I'll let you get to know the real me."

"I'm looking forward to that." A muscle in his jaw twitched. "Let's circle the outside, make sure there aren't any other breaches. As soon as the crime scene techs get here, we'll grab lunch, then I'll drop you at the office for your orientation meeting. The sheriff's leaving for Austin tonight, and I know she wants to see you before she leaves."

"Why's she going to Austin?"

"She's testifying there in a case we closed a while back. She might be gone most of the week."

Bree tried to open a side door that wouldn't budge. She glanced over her shoulder to find Noah sauntering along a few yards behind her. "Can you walk any faster? My stomach hasn't stopped growling since you mentioned lunch."

He quickened his step and passed her. "And here I thought you ran on attitude and opinions."

"Deputy Reed, you haven't seen one ounce of my attitude yet."

"Just one more thing to look forward to, Deputy Delgado." He smiled at her over his shoulder.

"Better be careful what you wish for." She meant it for Noah. But based on her inside tingles brought on by his smile, maybe *she* should keep it in mind, too.

Chapter Four

Noah slid into the red vinyl booth at the Busy B Café, returning several greetings that came his way. In his early twenties, he'd spent four years earning his degree in Houston, the largest city in Texas. Fourth largest in the United States. An enjoyable time for him, but in the end, small-town life and the close ties of family called to him. He returned to Resolute and had never looked back.

The Busy B was already near capacity, boasting a down-home din of conversation and the subtle clinking of cutlery on plates. Though his day had already been full, it wasn't quite noon yet. A bit earlier than Noah normally took lunch, but teased by the savory smells, he was starving.

"What's good here?" Bree studied the laminated menu.

"Everything. And make sure to save room for pie." Noah glanced past her shoulder. Marge, the Busy B's owner, made a beeline for them, coffeepot in hand. "Oh, and get ready."

Bree lowered her menu. "Ready for what?"

"A force of nature."

The *force of nature* was a rotund woman in her sixties with a tight gray perm and expressive caterpillar brows. The squeak of her orthopedic shoes as she shuffled across the black-and-white-checkered linoleum floor halted at their table. "How you folks doing today? No, don't answer that. I can plainly see you're both wrung out. Must've been dealing with that explosion. Heard it was drugs, and maybe some people died in the fire. Terrible thing." She tsked, then pointed to the empty mugs already on the table. "Now, pull them coffee cups a little closer, and let's recharge your batteries."

"Yes, ma'am." Noah complied without hesitation. He'd learned long ago there was zero point in arguing with Marge. In the end, she always had her way.

While she filled his cup, Noah tried to give Bree a look of warning, one that would guide her in dealing with Marge. But she missed it. Bree, it seemed, would have to learn to deal with Marge on her own. Noah sat back to watch the drama unfold.

"No coffee for me, thank you." Bree glanced back at her menu.

"Hon—" Marge set the pot on the table "—scoot your skinny backside over and make room for me."

Bree looked to him for help, but he gave her a small shrug that said, *Too late. You're on your own.*

Marge chuckled, obviously enjoying herself. "Go on, sugar. Scoot. I ain't gonna bite."

Bree slid over, if a bit reluctantly, and Marge squeezed

into the booth next to her. "I'm Marge, owner of this fine establishment. And you must be our newest deputy."

"I am." Bree's smile wavered, giving away her discomfort with the personal space violation. "Deputy Brianna Delgado."

Marge frowned. "Well, that won't do. Noah?"

"Bree," he supplied. Marge didn't cotton to formalities.

"Much better. Now, Bree, honey, when I told you to shove your coffee cup closer, I wasn't really asking. First off, it's colder than a well digger's belt buckle since that front blew in, and you need to stay warm. Second, it's clear as a bottle of vodka that you need to add some octane to that tank of yours."

How did one argue with that kind of logic? Bree moved her cup closer, and Marge poured. "Wouldn't hurt to stir in a good amount of sugar. Go on. It's right there."

While Bree reached for a couple of sugar packets, Noah sipped his black coffee. "Marge thinks diabetes is misinformation spread by sugar haters."

Bree smirked as Marge turned to him, brows pushed together in a frown. "It wouldn't hurt you none to have a little sugar, either, Mr. Smarty Pants. Might sweeten that vinegary disposition of yours."

"You know I love you." Noah gave Marge one of his most flirtatious smiles.

"Bah, you scoundrel." Marge winked at him, then turned her attention back to Bree. "Now you understand *one* of the reasons Cassie hired you. That department of hers already has far too much testosterone. You'll balance things out a bit. And for the better, if you ask me."

"Yes, ma'am. Seen that firsthand already." Bree gave Noah a pointed look.

Marge cackled. "Ha! Nailed it. Noah's the one in need of taming most of all."

"I'll do my best." Bree stirred her coffee.

"I'm holding you to that, young lady." Marge gave a motherly pat to Bree's hand, then touched one of her short, dark curls. "Why, aren't you just the cutest thing. So pretty, and like a breath of fresh air. Isn't she a peach, Noah?"

"Oh, yeah. She's a *real* peach." But a peach that doesn't look comfortable being touched.

"Honey." Marge turned back to Bree. "You just gotta ignore this boy when he gets all sarcastic like that. Heaven knows, I did my best with him, but he was motherless." She shook her head and tsked. "Means he's just one step up from a savage with his manners."

"Better not let Cassie catch you finding fault with her child rearing."

"Oh, that poor dear did her best, too. But she was a child herself, and some boys are just too stubborn to corral." Marge patted Bree's hand again. "Now then, little peach, heard you was from San Antonio."

"Born and raised." Bree eased her hand out from under Marge's and reached for the bowl of small creamer pods.

Noah could have sworn she used the motion to cover her annoyance with being touched. And maybe to try to hide the neutral mask that slipped unbidden over her face. *What secrets are you hiding, Brianna Delgado?*

Marge appeared not to notice. "Resolute must be quite the change from all that big-city hullabaloo."

"I thought it would be a quiet town, but today's been pretty exciting."

That produced a contemptuous snort from the older woman. "Reckon so. Imagine, people blowin' themselves up for drugs." Marge shook her head. "So, tell me, what made you decide to leave a big-city police force and come join our little sheriff's department?"

Bree shrugged, almost as if this was nothing more than a casual get-to-know-one-another conversation. But there was something about the set of her spine, the rigidity of her posture that told Noah this was anything but casual for her. Noah would bet money she was definitely hiding something.

"Oh, you know. Little fish. Big pond. Thought I might make a bigger splash in a smaller pond."

"Sound thinking, so long as you know that Resolute's more a puddle than a pond." Chuckling, Marge added, "But it's a beautiful puddle, and we love it. Drug dealers and explosions notwithstanding." Marge reached out to pat her hand again, but Bree must have seen it coming because she lifted her cup. "You'll see. I bet before long, you'll love it here, too."

Bree gave Marge one of her genuine smiles. "I'm sure I will."

"And I don't know about the folks you worked with in San Antonio," Marge went on, "but here, you'll be working with the best of the best."

Bree flashed him an inscrutable look. "Good to know."

Marge waved over Rachel. Wearing a blue polyester server uniform, the waitress hustled up to the table and set a coffee cup in front of her boss. "Need anything else, Marge?"

"Thanks, sweetie, but I'm just getting to know our new deputy while I give these barking dogs of mine a rest. This darling peach is Deputy Bree Delgado. Bree, Rachel Miller. Best waitress, mother and all-around person this side of the Pecos River."

Born in Resolute, Rachel was a thirtyish divorced mother of two and a fixture at the Busy B. She'd had a rough go of it the last year or so, and like the motherless Reed kids, Marge had taken her under her large and loving wing. The younger woman smiled warmly at Bree. "Nice to meet you, and welcome to Resolute."

"Thanks." Bree brandished another genuine smile. "Nice to meet you, too."

"What can I bring you?" Rachel pulled her pad and pencil from her apron pocket.

Noah and Bree gave Rachel their orders, and the nimble waitress took off like a race walker. Between rushing around the diner and having two small kids at home, it was little wonder she stayed beanpole thin.

"She seems very nice." Bree fiddled with another sugar packet but didn't open it.

"And capable." Marge's pleasant demeanor slipped. "You wouldn't know it to look at her, but a little over a year ago—while pregnant with her second child, no less—she caught her no-account drunkard of a husband in bed with another woman. Oh, he was a smooth talker, that one. Fooled us all. But you gotta give Rachel credit. Kicked his sorry butt to the curb and divorced him, just like that." Marge snapped her fingers. "Said she wasn't having nothing to do with a man who had the morals of an alley cat. Takes a strong woman to do that with a toddler at home and a newborn on the way."

"Rachel is definitely that," Noah said.

"What about you?" Marge asked Bree while pouring coffee for herself. Noah grimaced when she stirred in four packets of sugar. "Got a husband? Kids?"

Bree shook her head. "Never married, and no kids." She met Marge's twinkling eyes over the rim of her coffee mug. "And I'm not in the market for either."

"Oh, honey. That's what they all say." Marge's lips curved into a sly smile Noah knew all too well. She'd tossed it around with abandon when Bishop had first rolled into town last summer. As it turned out, Marge had been right about Cassie and Bishop, so there'd be no stopping her now if she aimed to find the perfect match for her "little peach." "Have you found a place to live yet?"

"I'm thinking about renting until I see how things go. For now, I'm staying at Doc's Motor Court." Bree shrugged. "Considering it looks like it was built in the 1950s, it's not bad. The owner suggested I take one of their stand-alone rooms in the back. It's fairly quiet."

"Those *are* the best rooms," Marge said, nodding, "but you let me know if you have any problems. I'll set Doc straight, make no mistake."

Bree arched a brow. "It's going to take me a while to

get used to everyone knowing everyone else. I gather you hold sway over Doc?"

"Why, of course I hold sway over him." Marge snorted. "I'm married to the old coot." Her contagious laughter spread to Bree. Marge leaned in, her voice now a loud whisper. "Hon, the real truth is, I hold sway over darn near everyone in this town 'cause I know all their secrets."

"Oh." Bree's face paled a little, and her cup clinked against the table as she picked it up with an unsteady hand.

Oh yes, Bree Delgado. You're definitely hiding something.

Rachel came back with their meals and was gone in a flash.

"Well, now." Marge smacked the flats of her hands on the table. "Reckon you two have some top secret deputy stuff to discuss, so I'll get back to work myself." She hefted herself from the booth with a groan. "Bree, darling, it was so nice to meet you. And if you ever find yourself in need of a break from that office full of men, come hang out here anytime you like." She headed toward the kitchen.

Noah rested his forearms on the table and smiled at Bree. "Like I said, a force of nature."

"I like her." She picked up her burger and took a bite.

"Hard not to. I tease, but she's good people." Noah shoved a fry into his mouth. "She also knows just about everything that goes on around here. When you're investigating anything, Marge should always be on your list of folks to interview."

"So, the town gossip."

"A gossip with integrity. If you tell her to keep something on the down-low, she will. To the grave."

Bree chewed and swallowed. "Good to know. Any other tips you want to share?"

"I'm sure I'll think of a few. I don't want to overwhelm you on your first day." He laughed when she rolled her eyes.

"Too late for that." Her lips curved into a genuine smile that warmed his insides like the slow burn from fine sipping whiskey. "But I'm sure your intentions were good."

He gave her a sheepish grin. "Didn't want you scurrying back to San Antonio, sorry you ever came here."

"No worries on that score." Bree's smile faded faster than a West Texas sunset dipping below the horizon. She turned her face from him—a sure sign she was lying—and glanced out the café window.

The list of things to learn about her grew, and Noah couldn't help but wonder. Why had she *really* left a promising career in San Antonio to become a deputy in one of the smallest counties in Texas?

His cell phone vibrated in his pocket, interrupting his musings. He checked the number before answering. "What's up, Helen?"

"I called on your phone because I know you're at lunch, and I don't want the whole diner hearing this. You need to get over to the McNultys'. I don't have anyone else available right now."

"Ah, man. Not again. Isn't this like the third time this month?"

"Yes, but this time it was Mrs. Parsons calling. I made her tell me everything that's going on before I'd agree to send a deputy." Noah listened to all the details.

"We're on our way." He ended the call, put away his phone and waved to Rachel. "Need these to go, please." He pointed at their lunches.

"Coming right up." Rachel brought the boxes to the table in record time.

"Thanks." Noah handed her his credit card and packed up his food while she dashed to the register.

Bree pushed her box off to the side, took one last huge bite of her burger and stood. "You don't have to pay for my food, you know."

"I know. I got this meal. You get the next one. Okay?"

She gave a one-shoulder shrug. "Okay."

Noah followed her toward the door, handing Rachel a cash tip and grabbing his card on the way out.

If Bree thought Marge was something, wait till she met the McNultys and Widow Parsons. Boy, oh boy. Their shift was only half over, and already it was turning out to be one heck of a day.

Chapter Five

Bree, stuffed after eating only half her burger, insisted on driving so Noah could finish his on the way. Also, she was already getting tired of riding shotgun. She'd had her own patrol car in San Antonio. Had driven when she wanted to and let her partner drive when she didn't. She had been in control.

But now, even though she had the wheel, she felt like a chauffeur. "Where are we going?"

Between bites, he directed her to a property about twenty minutes outside of town. Not quite a ranch, not even a big farm. Just a lot of land and several outbuildings behind a small wood-frame house.

As she put the car in Park, Noah gave her the lay of the land. "Ray and Ruth McNulty live here." He popped the last fry in his mouth, stuffed his napkin into the carryout container and pointed to another house down the road. "And over there is where Widow Parsons lives. Abby Parsons has been labeled by some people as a redneck trophy bride because she was so much younger than her husband. The kind of woman who always takes pride in her appearance, although I've heard it said she overdresses for every occasion." His mouth kicked up at the corners in a sheepish smile. "Anyway, after her husband died, Ray McNulty offered to help her with home repairs and the more strenuous physical labor needed on her property."

"Let me guess—the widow repaid Ray with her own version of physical labor."

Chuckling, Noah shrugged. "It's been one of the worst-kept secrets around here for a few years."

"The wife…?"

"Ruth."

"Right. So Ruth knows?"

"Yep, though admittedly, she was slow to catch on. But ever since she did, we've been dealing with the McNulty-Parsons feuds on a regular basis."

"*Feuds*, plural? Don't you mean the Ruth-Abby feud?"

"Well, yeah. The women have been at each other's throats for a hot minute. But there's also one heck of a lot of sparring between the two McNultys."

Bree blew out a long-suffering breath. "Why can't men just keep it zipped?" A problem her last boyfriend had had. He just couldn't keep his hands off the badge bunnies. Which was why she'd dumped his sorry butt over a year ago and swore she'd never date another cop. There hadn't been anyone in her life since, and she liked it that way. Uncomplicated. Bree totally got why Rachel threw her loser husband out.

"Hey, no fair generalizing. We're not *all* hound dogs."

"Uh-huh, sure." Bree twisted her mouth to the side. "So, what are we about to walk into?"

"You're gonna love this. Apparently, Ruth got ahold of Ray's cell phone and sent a text asking Abby to meet '*him*.'" He emphasized with air quotes. "Naturally, Ruth made sure to pick a time when she knew Ray wouldn't be home." Noah didn't bother hiding his mirth. He clearly found the whole situation amusing, and Bree wasn't sure what to make of that. As someone who had been hurt by infidelity, it wasn't a situation she normally found funny.

Noah went on. "Okay, here's where it gets good. Do you hear that honking—and maybe an occasional shriek?"

Bree cocked her head. Sure enough. "I do."

"The McNultys raise geese. Mean suckers, geese. At least, the domesticated ones are. Protective of their owners and can get vicious when guarding them against predators. Both real and perceived."

Bree opened the driver's-side door of the patrol car. "And for whatever reason, they think Abby is a predator."

"That they do, and they've got her surrounded on the back patio." Noah got out of the car wearing a devilish smirk. "Tell you what—since I know her, I'll talk to Ruth, try to get her to call off her birds. In the meantime, you see about dispersing the geese and getting Abby off the property."

"Wait. I'm a city girl. What do I know about handling geese?"

"About as much as I do. Just don't make them mad."

"Then why—"

Already closing the distance to the McNultys' front door, Noah shouted one word over his shoulder: "Newbie."

Okay, if that's the way you want to play it, fine. I can handle this.

Patio. Backyard. Bree headed along the side of the house.

I've taken down 250-pound street thugs. What's a few geese? Nothing more than glorified ducks, right? I'll flap my arms around, maybe yell at them, and they'll fly away. Job done.

She hesitated at the back corner of the house. The faint honking and shrieking was louder. She peeked around the corner and sized up the situation lickety-split.

An attractive, fortyish blonde was clearly dressed for a tête-à-tête in a low-cut, high-hemmed dress, though the fabric was ripped and her hair was askew. Several red welts marred her bare arms and legs; one was maybe bleeding. Hard to tell from this distance, but they all looked painful.

The widow had escaped the reach of her attackers by standing on top of the rickety patio table barefoot, her expensive-looking, shiny red high heels lying on the ground, covered in globs of goose poop. Abby Parsons might be a two-timing redneck trophy wife, but currently she was a hot mess in a terrible fix.

As reported, a flock of maniacal birds surrounded her. No, not a flock—a gaggle. A gaggle of strutting, neck-bobbing, wings a'flapping, honking and hissing, maniacal geese. Alfred Hitchcock couldn't have concocted a better scene.

As the assault continued, accompanied by the widow's occasional shrieks of profanity, poop flew everywhere. Even from Bree's distance, the droppings were like nothing any bird had ever left on her car. These were disgusting.

Bree approached at a snail's pace. "Ma'am, I'm Deputy Delgado of the Boone County Sheriff's Department, and I'm here to help you."

At the sound of Bree's voice, eight black-beaked heads with tiny, malevolent eyes turned their attention her way in unison. For a brief moment of silent hesitation, it seemed the creatures considered whether she was friend or foe.

Streaks of mascara running down her cheeks, the frazzled woman looked up, her relief palpable. "Oh, thank heavens."

The geese did not seem as pleased by Bree's arrival. A couple of the closest birds waddled in her direction, honking and flapping their wings. "That's close enough," Bree warned but was soundly ignored. The two kept coming. *What now?* She called on the strategic principle of the best defense being a good offense.

"Scram!" Waving her arms wide, she ran toward them.

Bad idea.

Instead of running away, they hissed, stretched out their wings and charged her, a few of their compatriots joining in.

Bree ran from the patio out onto the grassy yard, the

geese hot on her tail. Circling back toward the house, she shouted to the widow, "Why aren't they flying away?"

Ms. Parsons, busy kicking at the geese who were trying to bite her toes, stared at Bree. "Domesticated geese don't fly more than a few feet off the ground." With arms flailing, she managed to keep her balance, roll her eyes and smirk all at the same time. "Where on earth are you from that you don't know that?"

"San—ow!—Anto—get *away* from me!—nio— dammit, stop biting me!" Bree swung her arms behind her, trying to swat at the giant goose that kept ramming his beak into her butt. When she reached the patio, she about-faced and mad-dogged the whole stinking lot of them, making herself as big as possible and yelling at the top of her lungs.

"Stop!" Abby shouted. "That will only make them mad—"

As if Bree needed convincing, the biggest goose rose up from the ground, arched its neck high and clamped down on the closest thing to it: her right breast.

"Son of a..." The intense pain froze the scream rising in her throat. She pushed at the goose until it finally let go of her. More head-bobbing, wing-flapping and honking merged with the flow of expletives leaving Bree's mouth as she rubbed her sore nipple.

The big goose once again started toward her again. "I swear, you try it again and you're mine, mister. After what you did to me, I'll buy you from the McNultys. Don't care what it costs. You're gonna be my dinner *and* my pillow."

Several more birds joined Bree's current aggressor. Forming up like well-trained troops, they spread their wings and stretched their necks.

Then, as a unit, they charged.

Bree turned and ran across the patio. The biggest bird—had to be a male—got in one last painful jab as Bree scrambled up onto the table. Panting, Bree pressed the button on her shoulder mic. "Deputy Reed, this is Deputy Delgado requesting immediate assistance in the backyard."

Noah appeared darn near instantly. Judging by his idiotic grin, he'd been watching the goings-on for some time. Maybe the whole time. Aggravating man.

Bree's eyes narrowed into slits. "You say one word, and I'll pulverize you."

His deep, rich laughter made her feel alive, but she still wanted to kill him. When one of the geese turned and charged him, Bree thought she'd have her revenge. Instead, Noah retreated backward, never taking his eyes off the aggressive bird, and disappeared around the side of the house. The traitor.

Way to have my back, partner.

And darned if the bird didn't halt its pursuit of Noah and return to the patio table.

Glaring down at the stupid bird, Bree derived momentary satisfaction imagining a savory cooked-goose dinner, complete with a sprig of parsley on top of the golden brown feast. "You're this close." She held up her thumb and finger to demonstrate exactly how close. More honking and hissing showed just how unimpressed he was with her threat.

Noah returned a moment later with Ruth in tow. "Come on, Ruth. That's my partner up there on that table. You've had your fun. Now call off your birds."

Abby's hiss rivaled those from the geese. "I swear, Ruth McNulty, I'm going to—"

"Ms. Parsons, what say you hold off with the threats until Mrs. McNulty corrals the geese?" Noah's tone was serious, but he just couldn't hide his amusement.

"Don't see why I should have to." Ruth crossed her arms, looking like a recalcitrant child. "If she wasn't such a husband-stealer who—"

"Ruth!" Noah shouted over the growing din of poultry. "The geese. Now."

With one last glare at the alleged husband-stealer, Ruth walked off in a huff, her beloved gaggle waddling after her. Bree leaped from the table, not even caring at this point about all the goose crap she probably had mashed onto the soles of her shoes. Noah came over and held out a hand to help the disheveled Abby down.

"How'd y'all know to come rescue me?" Abby eyed her shoes, her lip curling in distaste at the goopy decorations left by the geese. "Those are ruined. And they cost a fortune. I ought to make that old biddy pay to replace them."

"Oh, I don't know. They might clean up." Noah glanced at Bree as if she knew the answer. When she shrugged, he added, "And it was Ray who called this in."

Abby's mouth pursed and her nose wrinkled. "That sorry coward. I called him, told him what was going on, and he said *he* was on his way to help me."

Clearly, Ray wanted no part of the cat fight, despite it being a mess of his own making. Bree crossed her arms, wincing when they pressed against her sore breast. Yes, Ray was a coward.

But Abby Parsons was in no way blameless. "You have no grounds to compel Ruth to pay for your shoes, since they were damaged when you trespassed on her property."

Abby glared at Bree. "I did not trespass. I was invited." Then, dismissing her, Abby turned to Noah and batted her lashes. "Would you be so kind as to give me a ride home, Deputy Reed?" Her syrupy southern accent thickened with each word.

Bree rolled her eyes, making sure it was a gesture Noah couldn't miss.

"Sorry, Ms. Parsons, but we've got another call. The geese are corralled, and you're just a short walk down the road."

"How do you expect me to walk all that way barefoot?" It was as if Scarlett O'Hara had been resurrected.

Noah earned brownie points when he didn't fall for the routine. "I don't expect you to walk barefooted, Ms. Parsons. I expect you to put on those shoes."

She looked at them, her eyes wide with horror. "I couldn't possibly."

Bree had had enough. She marched to the back wall of the house and grabbed the hose. She twisted the faucet and, with Noah looking on in bemusement and Abby in disbelief, she squeezed the nozzle, spraying the goop off the shoes from where she stood. To say there was overspray was an understatement. "There. Problem solved."

"Th-they're soaked. My dress is soaked. *I'm* soaked."

"But clean enough for you to get on home all by your little old self." Bree gazed across the property. "And if I were you, I'd get those shoes on and beat feet before Mrs. McNulty comes back with her feathered friends."

Abby tucked loose strands of hair behind her ear in a vain attempt to right her appearance. "What ever happened to 'Protect and Serve'?"

"That's a police motto, ma'am. 'Committed to Excellence' is the promise of the sheriff's department."

"Well, I would hardly call this little episode 'excellence.' I don't imagine anyone would."

Noah hooked his thumbs in his duty belt. "Well, now, I s'pose that's a matter of opinion."

Noah's supportive words filled Bree with an unexpected warmth. But then she checked herself. Why did she care about the validation of a man she'd known for only a matter of hours?

Ms. Parsons, apparently heeding Bree's advice, ceased arguing and took off at a clipped pace, barefoot and bedraggled, her spine rigid with anger, soggy shoes dangling from her hand.

Bree and Noah followed her to the McNultys' front yard and watched to make sure she made it to her front porch before heading back to their cruiser.

"Ooo, doggy. She was madder than a wet hen."

"Is that supposed to be funny?" Bree reached for the car door, pleased Noah was still giving her the wheel.

He slid into the passenger seat. "It was. A little bit funny. Admit it."

"I will not." Bree fished out the keys.

"You could've gone easier on her, you know."

"I could have, but I chose not to. You have a problem with that?"

"Not a bit. Just wondered if that's your general MO when dealing with the shenanigans of infidelity."

"If you're asking if I look the other way, no, I do not. I mostly believe that people who cheat get what they deserve." She cranked the engine.

"For what it's worth, I don't hold with infidelity, either."

"I'm sure your future wife will be very happy to know that, but why are you telling me?"

"You told me your view. Just thought I'd share mine." He scrubbed a hand across his face. "Look, I've had enough of the McNulty-Parsons drama for one day. Let's get out of here."

Bree turned and fixed him with her sternest look. "Not yet. We have unfinished business."

"Seriously?"

"Yeah, seriously. Don't even try to convince me you didn't see those stupid geese attacking me. You made it to the backyard way too fast when I radioed in. You were already at the corner of the house, watching."

Bigger than the Rio Grande, his stupid grin spread across his face again.

"I knew it. You better not have a video of it."

When he didn't deny it, Bree crossed her arms, a habit when angry. She immediately regretted it. "I don't know what hurts more, my backside or my boob."

"We can stop at the store and pick up some goose ointment."

"Oh, you're hilarious."

"For real." Noah erupted in laughter. "It's actually called goose grease. Good for the relief of minor aches and pains."

The man found humor in everything, and it was time for a dose of his own medicine. Leaning toward him and batting her lashes, she drawled as well as Scarlett herself. "Why, you know I'm just a little ol' city girl stuck out here in the big, bad country. Would you be ever so kind, Deputy Reed, as to drop me at the office?" Switching back to her normal voice, she added, "I think I'll see if the sheriff has someone else I can ride with."

"Wow. Already?" His grin still sparkled. "You need to wrangle yourself up a better sense of humor, Delgado."

Bree wore a small smile herself. "And you need to lasso yourself a more mature one, Reed."

She glanced at him, expecting at least a chuckle. Instead, his grin disappeared, and he turned his head to look out the passenger window. For the life of her, she could not get a read on him. And truth be told, it didn't matter. Forget his good looks. Ignore his soul-deep laughter. Mr. Happy-Go-Lucky wasn't her type.

To banish the aggravating man from her mind, she turned her musings to more important things.

How do I get back to the justice center from here?
And...

How exactly does one care for a goose-bit boob?

Chapter Six

Noah's vehicle idled out front of the justice center while he waited for Bree. She'd lingered after the morning briefing—something about a personal phone call she had to make. Since the explosion and goose shenanigans on Monday, they'd had two days of nothing but mundane calls and minor incidents. Days so tedious that under normal circumstances, eight hours would have felt like twelve. But with Bree riding shotgun, quitting time seemed to butt right up against starting time. He'd actually started to enjoy her company, despite her exasperating stubborn streak and outspoken opinions.

Noah chuckled. When Cassie had assigned him to ride with Bree, his disappointment had been obvious. No doubt she assumed he was still unhappy about it, and he hesitated to correct that misconception.

When Cassie was raising her brothers, she'd been big on learning experiences, character-growth experiences, it'll-be-good-for-you experiences. Last year, when she'd been appointed sheriff, she'd applied those methods at work. As long as Cassie thought Noah didn't want to do something, she'd make him do it for the *experience*. And he might be a jokester, but he was no dummy. If he couldn't work the meth-house explosion, partnering with Bree was the next-best option.

The passenger door opened, and Bree paused. She leaned down, picked up the goose feather Noah had left on her seat and then climbed in. Twirling the feather shaft between her thumb and finger, she cocked one questioning brow at him.

"A memento of our first day together."

Bree snorted. "I hope this came from the goose that goosed me."

He backed out of the parking space. "Besides never yelling at or charging a goose, you should *never* try to pull a feather out of a live one."

"You could have told me about the charging and yelling *before* I had to deal with them," Bree muttered as she buckled her seat belt.

"I told you not to make the geese mad." He fought to keep his face straight as he put the car in Drive.

"Details would have been nice." She bent her head over the feather, inspecting it up close. "It's kind of pretty, the light gray color and then these darker dots making a design toward the tip."

"They're supposed to be lucky, too."

Bree looked at him. "What kind of luck are you hoping for?"

"Oh, I don't know." Noah headed east. "Maybe a little more on-the-job action."

"I see." A small frown formed as she set the feather

on the dash. "Monday wasn't enough excitement for one week?"

"You didn't think the last couple of days were boring?" He took his eyes off the road to look at her, but she kept staring straight ahead. "You're not missing the fast pace of your last job?"

"As a matter of fact, I'm not." She crossed her arms. He'd already caught on to that being a sign she was vexed about something or other. "And I doubt I'll be disappointed, since we're just going back to the high school, right?"

"Right." He stopped at one of the few red lights in Resolute and looked at Bree. "I got the forensics report this morning right after our meeting. No viable prints, no evidence collected except broken glass and the cheap padlocks cut off the storage areas in the gym. They compared the tool marks to a variety of possible bolt cutters, and apparently the ones used were as cheap as the locks." The light turned green, and he continued through the intersection. "But based on their findings, you were right—it was an inside job. We need to get a list from Principal Jackson of everyone with a key for that door, or a master key, and then—"

Helen's voice came over the police radio. "Reed and Delgado. What's your location?"

Noah grabbed the radio mic off the dash. "This is Reed. En route to Resolute High."

"Detour immediately to Peake's Sweets and Treats. Major disturbance in process. Subject is not armed but extremely violent. Upon arrival, advise if you need backup."

"On our way." He pulled to the side of the road and checked for traffic, then made a U-turn and sped back the way they'd come, lights and siren running.

"Peake's Sweets and Treats?" Bree asked.

"Ice-cream and candy shop about a block off the town square. Family-owned for generations. Bob Peake retired a few years ago, and now his daughter, Sandy, runs it. She's in her thirties. Super-nice lady, but she doesn't brook any trouble in the store."

The shop sat in the middle of a block of attached stores. Noah braked to a stop directly in front, angled in toward the curb. He killed the lights and siren, and they jumped from the car and approached the shop's windows, evaluating the situation.

"Looks like the place has been trashed. I only see one perp, left side, watching us."

"Several customers at the tables along this wall." She indicated the side closest to the door. "Adults *and* kids."

"And that's Sandy between the perp and the others, swinging a broom at him."

"She's got spunk." Bree stepped back from the window. "Think the back door is unlocked? If it is, we can come at him from both directions."

"No idea. How fast can you run?"

"Fast."

"Go."

In less than a minute, Bree was there and back.

"Locked." She sucked in deep breaths.

"Okay, let's do this." Noah pulled open the front door

and walked in, Bree right behind him. "Heard you're having some trouble, Sandy."

"I won't be if you'll hold him so I can whack him." She brandished the broom like a martial arts fighting staff.

The troublemaker was backed up against a wall with the non-business end of the broom. He was emaciated to the point that he resembled a clothed skeleton. Even from several feet away, sores on his face stood out against the pale skin stretched tight across his skull. He definitely *looked* like a meth addict. But that didn't jibe with the apparent sugar craving. That was usually associated with opioids or heroin withdrawal.

"I'm Noah. What's your name?" He took a step closer. Behind him, Bree urged the customers to leave *now*.

The man bounced from foot to foot. Noah estimated the guy's age to be midtwenties, though he looked older. Hard drugs were definitely not a body's friend.

"His name's Kenny." Sandy still stood nearby, brandishing her broom. "He's been in here before for candy, and I figured he was on heroin or oxy. I've never seen him like this."

"Well, Kenny, looks like you're upset about something." Noah stepped over downed spinner racks and what had to be hundreds of bags of candy, staying alert, ready for anything. As weak as the guy appeared, meth-induced psychosis could make him aggressive. "I'd like to help you work it out, if I can."

"She wouldn't let me have my candy." Kenny waved at Sandy.

"You were sticking your filthy hands in all the bins of loose candy," Sandy said, raising her voice. Her face turned almost as red as her hair. "Then slobbering all over your fingers and sticking them in more bins. I have to throw out my whole inventory thanks to you."

"Sandy," Bree said, "why don't you check on your customers outside while Noah talks to Kenny?"

Sandy cursed under her breath at Kenny but must have listened to Bree, because the front door opened and closed.

"If all you want is candy, we can fill up some bags for you." Noah kept his voice calm. "That sound good?"

Kenny studied the two deputies with dilated eyes, scratched at one of the scabs on his face and then charged Noah.

Raising his arms, Noah took a step back to brace himself. His right ankle rolled to the side, and he glanced down at a bag of monster jawbreakers beneath his foot. At the same moment, Kenny straight-armed him dead center in the chest. Noah's legs tangled in spinner racks that crisscrossed each other on the floor. His backward momentum slammed him into Bree, taking her down with him.

Kenny pointed at them, shrieked something about impostors and ran behind the counter.

"You okay?" Noah asked Bree while disengaging rack hooks that were caught in his clothes.

Pushing herself to her feet, Bree wiped blood from her lower lip, then helped pull Noah up from the floor. She touched the back of her head and winced. "I'll be fine, but Kenny seems to be spiraling."

As he tested his weight on his twisted ankle, Noah watched Kenny. The cash register sat on the counter beside cases filled with truffles and specialty candies. A few feet behind it, a cold case held tubs of ice cream, and next to that sat cones and toppings for sundaes and other icy creations. Having thrown open the cold-case lids, Kenny paced back and forth, shoving his arm down, then raising it with his hand full of ice cream. It melted and ran down his arm as he shoved his fingers into his mouth.

Satisfied his ankle wasn't sprained, Noah signaled for Bree to approach one end of the counter while he headed to the other. Kenny screamed incoherent words at them and faced off with Noah. Bree circled the end of the candy case and picked up speed. But her foot hit a puddle of melted ice cream and she went down, sliding into Kenny's legs like a bowling ball knocking down a seven-ten split.

Facedown in the sticky mess on the floor, Kenny struggled to get up. But Bree held his legs while Noah cuffed the troubled man, who then refused to get up. Unable to get traction in the melted ice cream, they pushed Kenny around the end of the counter and to a relatively clean area. They finally hoisted him to his feet and set him in a booth.

"I don't understand what's happening around here." Noah studied the wreckage. "Human traffickers and drug dealers last year, now a meth house exploding and an addict destroying the candy store." He shook his head. "What's next?"

"I don't know." Bree shrugged. "But we should probably get him into the car while he can still walk. Hard to say how long ago he used, and I don't feel like carrying his sorry butt if he comes down."

Noah agreed as he grabbed the guy by one arm and Bree got his other.

As they approached the shop's door, Sandy pulled it open from outside and held it for them. They got Kenny into the back seat of their vehicle, locked it up and then returned to the store.

Sandy stood in the center of the shop, hands planted on her hips as she surveyed the destruction of property and loss of inventory. "Thanks, Noah. If y'all hadn't gotten here when you did, *I* might've been the one getting arrested." She scoffed. "What a mess." She picked up a tipped-over rack.

"I know you probably want to jump in and clean up so you can get back to business, but first you need to take pictures." Noah glanced around. "Lots of pictures. Your insurance company will want them for the claim. And if you email them to me, I'll make sure they stay with the file. They'll show the extent of the damage when he goes to court."

Sandy sighed but set the rack back to its overturned position.

"Can I ask how all this started?" Bree asked.

"Well, it started out as a glorious day here in the magical Land of Sweets, with rainbow candies and unicorn farts—" Bree's expression turned incredulous, and Sandy laughed, picking up a bag of Unicorn Farts cotton candy from the floor "—when suddenly, the meth monster breached the moat."

Still looking at the unicorn bag in Sandy's hand, Bree joined in with genuine laughter. It warmed Noah in a way he couldn't describe.

"It was pretty much what I said before. When he came in, he started grabbing loose candy from the bins without using the scoops. I yelled at him, and he came at me." Her mouth twisted into a smirk. "I grabbed the broom and got in a few good smacks with the bristles before I had to turn it around and poke him with the handle."

"Sorry I missed that." Noah laughed.

"I was impressed with your broom-combat skills," Bree said.

"You weren't so bad in the ice-cream wrestling pit, yourself." Sandy nodded toward Bree. "You must be the deputy Cassie was talking about hiring."

Bree stilled and her brows drew together as if she was uneasy at being the hot topic around town. But why?

"Sandy, this is Deputy Bree Delgado. Bree, Sandy Peake. And Bree, you shouldn't be surprised that so many people already know about you. It wasn't exactly a secret we were short a deputy."

"Pleased to meet you, Bree." Sandy beamed at both of them. "You and Noah make a good team."

"Oh, we're not really…" Bree's voice faded away as her cheeks took on a peach hue.

Noah cleared his throat at the awkward moment. Awkward for Bree, at least. *He* hoped they'd remain a team, even after Cassie returned from Austin. "Sandy, after you take the pictures, can you lock up and go over to the station to make a statement about what happened before we got here? Your insurance company is going to want that info, too. I'll add it to my report when I write it up later." He blew out a breath. "Right now we have to haul our friend to the hospital."

Sandy's eyes narrowed. "That jerk better not get off on some lame insanity plea just because he fried his brain with drugs. Not after what he's costing me."

"You do have business insurance, don't you?" Bree asked.

"Oh, sure we do. With a big fat deductible." Sandy rubbed her forehead. "And when Daddy finds out about this…"

"Don't worry—we're arresting Kenny." Noah didn't envy Sandy her situation. "But right now he needs to be cuffed to a hospital bed while they confirm what he's on. We always have to test for drugs and alcohol when we suspect the perp is under the influence. And there's no question with Kenny."

Sandy hmphed but seemed pleased by his words. "You might want to think about hog-tying him for the drive. Even if he crashes from the drugs, the sugar high will probably keep him buzzing for days." She pulled her phone from her pocket and started snapping pictures, muttering words that would make an oil rig roughneck blush.

BREE FIDGETED ON the hard-plastic hospital chair in the emergency room triage. Drumming her fingers on her knees, she waited for toxicology reports on Kenny

Schneider—according to the driver's license in his wallet—while Noah handled the hospital paperwork.

With wrists and ankles cuffed to the gurney, Kenny now lay quiet, sedated after still being out of control when they brought him in. Everyone knew the idiot was fried out on meth, but they would need the official findings for the criminal proceedings.

Plus, she had dealt with her fair share of addicts, and she'd bet the family-size M&M's stashed in her go bag that this guy was operating on more than one drug. As soon as his lab work was back, they'd haul his scrawny butt to jail and book him for multiple charges. Including assaulting two deputies.

Bree's body ached from the Sweets and Treats altercation. She must have smacked the floor when Noah slammed into her, based on the throbbing knot on the back of her head and accompanying killer headache. At least her lip had stopped bleeding, but it was tender.

Noah parted the curtains and entered the small space. "Heard anything yet?"

"They must still be running tests. By the way, I hope you're happy that your stupid feather gave you exactly what you wished for." In a mimicking voice she added, "'A little more action. A little excitement.'"

He grinned. "Never doubt the value of a goose feather." His expression sobered. "But seriously, you were impressive today, getting all the customers out safely. Especially the kids."

She dropped her gaze. "Yeah. The kids." Kids lost in the system. Kids needing a chance. Kids risking their lives by being on the streets, in a convenience store at the wrong moment, in a frickin' small-town candy store. When she looked up, she caught Noah studying her with those intense brown eyes of his. When he worked at it—like now—he seemed able to read her mind. She needed to shut that down, immediately. "You also gotta admit, I'd make a mean steer wrangler."

That broke his keen focus on her. "Remind me to take you to the Chute sometime." The corner of his mouth kicked up in a lopsided grin. "Best steaks in the county."

She frowned, confused by his left turn in the conversation. "I think I'm missing the connection between—"

"Help! Someone help me!" A woman's frantic yells brought Bree to her feet.

Noah yanked the curtain back that opened onto the ER lobby, but he and Bree remained where they were as nurses and orderlies ran to meet a woman carrying a child in her arms. A gurney appeared and a nurse helped the woman lay the small boy on it.

"He was playing in front of the house next door. By the grass ditch near the street." The woman sucked in a shaky breath. "Next time I looked, he was lying on the ground. I ran out there and found him having a seizure." Her fingers fluttered near the boy's face. "He threw up and I had to clear his throat."

"Has he had seizures before?" the nurse asked.

"No. Never." Her tears came faster. "I put him in the car and came as fast as I could. But by the time I got here, he was unconscious."

"Is he on any medications?" The nurse had two fingers on the side of the boy's neck as she glanced up.

The boy's mother shook her head.

"Okay, I've got a pulse. Let's get him into triage." The nurse turned back to the woman. "What's his name?"

"Joey. Joseph." She smacked the tears off her cheeks with the back of her hand, the sting seeming to calm her down some. "We call him Joey."

"I've already paged the doctor." Another nurse helped steer the gurney into the space next to their prisoner's.

Bree pulled the privacy curtain between the two beds open partway, and her breath caught as they removed the child's shirt, exposing his thin chest. It barely moved as he struggled for breath. After confirming his throat was clear, one nurse used a manual resuscitator to push air into his lungs as another wrapped a small blood pressure belt around his arm and clamped an oxygen monitor on his finger.

A doctor rushed into the tight space, and one of the nurses addressed the mother: "Ma'am, you should step out and let us work."

Bree had already consoled too many mothers whose children had overdosed—and stood in for even more who couldn't bother to be around for their kids, even in death. But when this woman's fear-filled eyes met hers, Bree went to her. Putting her arm around the woman's shoulders, she said, "Come stand with us over here." Thankful that the woman shuffled along with her, Bree tried to catch her eye. "What's your name?"

"Cindy."

Noah pulled the side curtain the rest of the way open so she could watch her son as a conversation ensued between the medical staff.

"Did he ingest anything? Come in contact with any contaminants? Cleaning products, maybe?" the doctor asked.

A nurse said, "We don't know."

Exasperated with the nurse, Bree spoke up. "Why on earth would you send his mother, who might be able to answer these questions, out of the room and then stand here unable to tell the doctor what he needs to know?" With her arm still around Cindy's shoulders, Bree moved her a large step closer to her son.

"I… He had a seizure before losing consciousness. He's never had one before." Cindy's voice gained volume. "I don't know if he came in contact with anything or ate anything—but if he did, it wasn't in the house."

Another nurse was cutting off the child's pants after removing his shoes and socks. "He's got what look like burns on his skin. Check his arms."

"They're on both forearms, too."

Everyone leaned in to see.

"He wasn't near any fire." Cindy's voice shook.

"These look like chemical burns. I want blood and urine right now. Complete lab workup." The doctor glanced at Cindy. "Was he playing with anything when you found him?"

"Just his ball." She paused. "There was a backpack near him in the ditch, but I barely noticed it."

Bree gave Cindy's shoulder a comforting squeeze. "Close your eyes and remember the backpack. Was it open or closed?"

"Um, I don't…" Her tear-soaked lashes fluttered shut for a moment before flying open again. "I remember!" Wide pools of blue bored into Bree's eyes. "It was open. There were things lying on the flap. And around it in the ditch."

"What things?" Bree kept her voice soft. "Picture them in your mind."

A frown took over the woman's face, and she closed her eyes again. "Plastic bottles. Funny-shaped papers. I think I saw a glove." Her eyes opened and she pointed at the blue nitrile gloves the medical staff wore. "A glove like those."

Bree signaled Noah to replace her arm with his. She crossed over to where the doctor stood, on the far side of the gurney. "Doctor." He gave her a quizzical look, and she leaned closer to him. "Check for acetone, ethyl alcohol, iodine crystal poisoning—any other chemicals used in meth production. The skin burns may be from opened lithium batteries or drain cleaner, maybe even lye."

The doctor's gaze bounced from Bree to the boy's mother and back. "You think she cooks meth?" he asked, his voice so low Bree barely heard it.

"No. I think someone dumped a backpack full of meth trash in that ditch."

The doctor raised his voice as he looked at the nurses. "Neither one of you leave this boy. Monitor his heart and lungs…"

Bree stopped listening to the doctor as she walked back to Noah and Cindy.

"What did the doctor say?" Cindy grabbed hold of Bree's hand. "Do you know what's wrong with my Joey?"

"I don't, but the doctor and nurses will keep you informed while they run tests. And I'm sure they won't mind you staying with Joey." Behind the woman's back, she poked Noah and motioned for him to move as far away as possible. She edged Cindy into her son's room and started to close the curtain. "I'm sorry, but we have to check on our patient now, and I don't want him to disturb you."

Bree met Noah on the far side of their prisoner's gurney and whispered directly into his ear, "You should call Chief Deputy Reed, suggest he have a hazmat tech collect that backpack and surrounding contents. Since the Austin crime lab covers Boone County, I guess they'll take it there to examine."

Noah raised his brows.

"I've seen this before. Meth cookers are notorious for dumping their toxic trash with no regard for who might happen upon it. Once I heard his mother's description of the backpack's items, I realized that was possibly the case here."

"Just from plastic bottles and weird papers?"

"I'll bet you my certified official *Lone Ranger* silver bullet those papers are coffee filters. They use them to strain their product."

Noah's cheeks puffed as he exhaled. Pulling out his phone, he paused, tapping his finger against its edge.

Bree sensed his frustration but held her tongue. On her first day, she'd noticed how much he wanted to work the meth explosion. He was probably thinking this might be a way into the investigation for him. Just drive to Cindy's and collect the backpack from the ditch as evidence. But instead of grabbing the opportunity, he punched in a speed dial number and followed the chain of command.

Good thing, since she didn't want to be exposed to possible meth toxins if she went with him. Or accused of ignoring protocol by leaving their detainee alone, cuffed to his gurney. Or involved in any high-profile drug-murder investigation. If a child died by meth poisoning, that's exactly what they'd have, and it was something she needed to avoid. Sitting in the hospital with a brain-fried sugar freak seemed the better option for her right now.

Just keep your head down, Delgado. Head down, mouth shut. And you might get out of this mess before your secret is revealed.

Chapter Seven

Bree relaxed after finding out Sean Cavanaugh, the deputy with the military bearing, would maintain the chain of custody on the backpack until a crime tech from Austin arrived to take possession.

Still waiting for the tox screen on Kenny Schneider, she and Noah cooled their heels in the small triage space, sharing a vending machine bag of pork rinds and arguing whether Coke or Dr. Pepper should be the Texas state drink. Once you got past sweet tea, Lone Star beer and top-shelf tequila, that is.

When the blood work came back revealing not only methamphetamine but also traces of heroin in their prisoner's system, they hauled him to the justice building's jail and tucked him away in a cell.

"You want to write up the reports now?" she asked Noah.

"I'm starving, and I was supposed to meet Bishop a half hour ago for lunch."

"Bishop?" Bree asked.

The corners of his mouth curved up in a smile. "My eventual brother-in-law, if my stubborn sister ever agrees to set a date. Meet you back here in an hour? After we finish the reports, we'll need to meet with Adam."

"Works for me."

Under different circumstances, Bree might have enjoyed sitting across from Noah's handsome face and getting to know him better. But considering she had no intention of taking part in the getting-to-know-you's, she was glad to have her lunch hour to herself.

She settled into a booth at the Busy B and opened the *Boone County Bulletin*. Tonight she'd look online for a place to rent, but she'd noticed a stack of *Bulletins* near the diner's front door and figured she'd take a look while she ate. The classified ads included listings for everything from babysitting jobs wanted to crocheted dog clothes for sale. She rolled her eyes at the picture of a poodle in a hooked-yarn dress.

She snapped the paper open to another page and folded it back. She would've been okay with an apartment since she had never planned on staying long. But there was only one complex in, or even near, Resolute. She'd checked out the Oak View Apartments when she met Sheriff Reed for her first interview.

The bulk of the occupants were elderly, living in that undesirable purgatory between their own home and a nursing home. The others seemed to be transient construction workers, living paycheck to paycheck and renting by the month. The building reeked of dead-end despair and end-of-the-road depression.

Which left Bree with only one option. She located the "Houses for Rent" section in the *Bulletin*. With no idea exactly where any of them were located, she drew circles around each possibility with her red pen. She'd look them up later on her map app.

Sensing movement next to her, she looked up to find Rachel holding a tray. She shoved her paper, pen and phone off to the side to make room for her lunch.

"Sorry it took so long. Marge is training a new cook." Rachel set down Bree's club sandwich and fries. "Looking for anything in particular?" She indicated the paper as she refilled the empty iced-tea glass.

"Right now I'm staying at Doc's, but it's temporary. I'd considered going into an apartment, but there's not much available in that category around here, is there?" With any luck, there were more she didn't know about.

Rachel gave her a smiling shrug. "Not so much, no."

Bree muttered a curse beneath her breath. She still wasn't used to small-town realities. She picked up the *Bulletin.* "I guess that leaves me with renting a house, but I'm not familiar with the layout of the town." She nodded toward the red circles.

"Let me see." Rachel took the paper from her. After skimming through the circled listings, she shook her head. "You don't want any of these. Some of them are way out of town. Others aren't in the best areas. Like this one here." She held the paper in front of Bree and pointed. "That's in an industrial area, mostly ware-houses." She inched her nail over to the next column. "And this one is in Flowertop."

"Where's Flowertop?" Bree mumbled around a bite of sandwich.

"A fair drive to the west. You should be able to find

something nice a whole lot closer." Rachel set the paper on the table. "Truth is, most things listed in this paper aren't usually worth checking out."

"I thought that might be the case when I saw the basset hound wearing a pink crocheted tutu."

Rachel barked out a laugh. "Some people around here don't have a spare second, and others have too much time on their hands." She lowered her voice. "Or a lack of respect for our four-legged friends."

Nodding her agreement, Bree sighed. "I guess I'll go back to my original plan and look online tonight."

Rachel snapped her fingers. "I may have a solution for you." She pulled her phone from her uniform pocket and fiddled with it as she spoke. "When my ex's parents passed away, I found this Realtor who also flips houses. He bought their house as is and made everything so easy for us. I can give you his name and number. He should know all the properties for sale or rent around Resolute. He's also not too hard on the eyes." She gave Bree a sly smile. "What's your number?"

Bree gave Rachel her number and a moment later the Realtor's info was in her contacts.

"Save my number, too. Give me a call if you want me to come with when you go looking at places. Fair warning—between my hours here, my kids and life in general, I probably won't be able to make it. But I've heard miracles happen. No, wait. That was in a Disney movie, wasn't it?"

"No kids, so I haven't seen a lot of those." Bree smiled. "Thanks for the help. This may save me a lot of time. But please don't tell Marge about the handsome Realtor, or I suspect she'll try to set me up with him."

Rachel laughed again. "You've got our Marge pegged, that's for sure. Don't worry—your secret is safe with me."

It was only a joke, but secrets seemed to be dominating Bree's life these days, and she didn't like it.

Rachel looked toward the front of the cafe. "I'd better get moving before Marge starts looking for me and discovers that you're dying for a date with the Realtor."

Bree's eyes popped open wide. "Oh, you're so bad."

"Sorry. Couldn't help it," Rachel said with an amused smirk.

Chuckling, Bree checked the time on her phone. "Could you bring me a to-go box? I don't have time to finish my sandwich here, but it's too good to leave behind."

"Be right back." Rachel tucked the tray under one arm and worked her way past the other tables, filling glasses with tea.

A warm happiness swept through Bree that had nothing to do with good food or finding a Realtor. Rachel had bantered with her as if she was someone, um, normal. Not like someone to be wary of, someone who carried a gun. In San Antonio, Bree's only friends had been on the force, and even they hadn't been close. She'd told herself it didn't matter, and for the most part, that was true. The job sustained her. Always had. But just now, the simple exchange with Rachel stirred up a big old pot of "wouldn't that be nice."

I think I just made a friend. So there, Deputy Reed. How was that for finding a black cat in a coal cellar?

AFTER PICKING UP a fried-oyster po' boy and Coke from the Seafood Shack, Noah drove to Bishop Investigations. Business for the private investigator had been steady since Bishop had moved to Resolute from Houston. Helping to solve a human-trafficking case last summer had helped, and word of mouth took it from there.

"Hey, you're late. Wasn't sure you'd make it." Bishop rose from his desk chair and went to his not-so-mini mini-fridge.

"My mundane, on-schedule morning got derailed by a last-minute service call." Noah pulled a visitor chair closer to the desk and made himself comfortable. As he unwrapped his sandwich and spread out the paper to catch drippings, he inhaled a deep breath of fried saltwater ambrosia. "Been working anything interesting lately?"

The disgustingly health-conscious Bishop sat across from him and opened a container of homemade kale salad. Blueberries, chopped apples and chunks of nuts sat on top of it, along with what looked like a pile of bird seed. How he and Cassie managed to coexist was beyond Noah.

"A case over in Houston. Looking for heirs of a very rich, very prolific man. The named heirs in his will want the estate settled before any more offspring are located. I made the mistake of driving there on Tuesday to talk to a possible son, but the guy was an impostor. When he looked like a sure thing, I'd stopped with the background checks and wasted almost two days. Now I'm going to research every possible descendant to death before going back to interview them." He poured something green that Noah hoped was dressing on his salad. "How's the new deputy working out?" Bishop mixed the bowl of salad with his fork.

His mouth filled with a large bite of sandwich, Noah took the opportunity to analyze the week so far. He swallowed. "She's not bad."

"Cassie said she's cute." Bishop's eyes never left Noah's face as he forked kale into his mouth. "That true?"

Noah set his sandwich down and grabbed a napkin to wipe the tartar sauce off his fingers. "Yeah, definitely cute. She has the most amazing eyes, like blue ice. And she's observant. Good at the job."

Taking a long drink of green tea from his clear travel mug, Bishop continued to watch him. "Blue ice, huh? Did you know that's the strongest type? Gets its color and strength from how it's formed with no air bubbles."

"Interesting." Not how the ice formed but how it applied to Bree. Strong.

"So what's on the flip side?" Bishop picked up a piece of walnut with his fingers and popped it into his mouth. "She can't be perfect."

"Oh, trust me, she's not." Noah leaned against his chair back. "She's stubborn as all get-out. And contrary?" He scoffed. "I explain why we do things a certain way here, and she just wants to argue."

"And yet…?"

"I can't stop thinking about her." He wadded up his

napkin and tossed it on the desk. "But she won't open up. She has stories she won't tell, secrets she's keeping. It's frustrating."

Bishop shrugged. "So take her to dinner or something. Let her know you're interested in getting to know her." He snapped the lid onto his salad container. "You aren't usually this discombobulated about asking someone out. Even though it hasn't even been a week, sounds like you're developing feelings for her."

"It's not that simple." Noah dropped his head back and groaned at the ceiling. "First off, we work together. Plus, Cassie already thinks I'm a goof-off. I'm trying to up my game on the job to prove myself to her." He looked at Bishop. "Hitting on the new deputy—the only other female in the department besides Cassie—won't win me any points. She'll figure I'm paying more attention to Bree than the job." He blew out a hard breath. "That's really the problem. I have to choose between the job and the girl, and the job's what's always been important to me."

"Sounds like you've got yourself a gen-u-ine conundrum." Bishop tipped back in his chair and rested his boots on the corner of his desk. "Wanna meditate on it?"

Noah summoned as much indignation as he could and crammed it into his reply. "No, I don't want to *meditate* on it, you hippie freak. That's probably why Cassie won't set a wedding date."

"Ha. Guess she hasn't told you she started doing yoga with me." A satisfied smile took over Bishop's face. "You ever hear of couples' yoga? Some of the positions are—"

"I don't need to hear about that." He gathered up his lunch trash and tossed it in a waste basket. "Anyway, everything I said stays between us, right?"

With a phony frown, Bishop nodded. "Oh, absolutely. I would never tell the person I cherish most in the world any of the dumb stuff her brother shares with me."

"I'm serious, man." Noah pointed a finger at him. "If she thinks—"

"Relax, Noah. I don't tell anyone what you tell me in confidence." He raised his brows. "If I did, I couldn't blackmail you later."

"Funny. Very funny. See y'all Saturday for dinner."

"Yep. Cassie confirmed she'll be home for the weekend. She's not happy about how long the trial is dragging on."

"Can't say I blame her. Doubt I could sit there for a whole week, just to find out I have to do it again next week." Noah opened the office door to leave.

"Don't worry about her being in a bad mood and taking it out on you." Bishop waited until Noah turned around. "I'll make sure she's relaxed several times over before dinner."

"She's my sister, you weirdo. I don't want to hear that stuff." Noah tried to slam the door behind him as a final last word. Instead, he cursed the soft-close hinges for denying him the satisfaction.

ON HIS WAY back to the office, Noah detoured to the high school and picked up the list of people with access to the school's keys. Once he and Bree were done with the candy-store incident, they could get back to the burglary.

When he walked into the bullpen, he found Bree sitting at his desk, takeout from the Busy B spread out in front of her. "Sorry, but this one's mine." He pointed to the desk where Adam used to sit. "That one's yours."

She looked over at Dave, sitting a couple of places over from her. "Why didn't you say something when I sat down?" When he only shrugged, Bree rolled her eyes. Then to Noah, "I didn't realize they were assigned." She dropped the french fry she'd been holding onto a paper towel and started to collect her ketchup packets and napkins. "I didn't have time to finish my lunch at the diner. I put my sandwich in the fridge but figured I'd eat the fries before they got too soggy."

"Never mind. Just stay there for now." Noah walked over to what had been Adam's desk. Bree hadn't spent much time in the pen this week, and everyone else was in and out. It made sense she hadn't known each deputy had their own spot. "Go ahead and finish your lunch. I'm going to get started on the candy-store report."

Dave laughed. "Figures you'd let a little thing like her boss you around, Reed."

Almost from Dave's first day, he'd harassed Noah. Cassie had attempted to curb Dave's behavior and stop his constant sniping at everyone else. But Dave got cagier, only heckling the other deputies when she and Adam were out of earshot. It was like dealing with a tiresome school bully, and Noah ignored the taunt, just as he always ignored whatever came out of Dave's mouth. Bree, on the other hand, was on her feet before he'd finished talking.

She stalked across the room and stopped next to

Dave, her narrowed eyes glinting. "First of all, it's not appropriate to mock a deputy with seniority over you."

Dave snickered. "And what's second of all, little lady?"

"Don't ever refer to me as a 'thing' again. I'm not a thing *or* a little lady to you. I'm your coworker. A deputy. And you'll refer to me as such."

Noah sat in his chair and watched, a smile plastered on his face. Dave was about to make things so much worse for himself.

"Or what?" The confident sneer he usually reserved for Noah appeared.

She leaned over his desk. "Or one of two things can happen." Noah was pleased to see Dave flinch as Bree held up a finger inches away from his face. "One, I'll punch those pearly whites of yours down your throat, hold your nose and watch you choke."

"I'd like to see you try."

Bree went on as if he hadn't spoken. "Or two, I inform our boss—the by-the-book, forward-thinking female sheriff—about your misogynistic attitude and lack of respect toward your fellow officers."

Dave's look turned mutinous.

"Now, I've only been here a week, so I don't know you very well, but I'd say it's a crapshoot on which would be more painful." The hand in front of Dave's face curled into a fist. "But you look like a man whose head could take a licking better than his pride, so why don't I call this one for you?" In a flash, Bree adjusted her feet and cocked her arm back, her chest turned in such a way that showed she knew exactly how to put her body behind a forceful right hook.

Dave realized it, too, because he raised his arms in front of his face. Not to fight, but to protect said pearly whites.

Noah jumped to his feet, closed the space between them and grabbed her arm. "Bree, as much as I hate to, I can't let you do that. You have an unfair advantage over poor old Dave. The rest of us have noticed that he hides from physical confrontations, so I doubt this would be a fair match. And as sorry an excuse for a deputy as he may be, Cassie doesn't have time to find another new one right now."

Her arm relaxed and she turned to Noah, her eyes now sparkling with amusement. "I understand. I'd hate to have Cassie upset with me during my very first week."

She returned to Noah's desk, packed up her lunch and relocated to what was now her own.

"She's a psychopath," Dave whispered to Noah, loud enough for her to hear.

"You better believe it," Bree stage-whispered back, staring at Dave with disturbingly wide eyes and an evil grin.

Noah left the room until he could control his laughter. Then he got back to work, trying to focus on the report he needed to type up instead of on Bree. The more time he spent with her, the more she fascinated him. When he first met her, he'd found her pretty. Or was it cute?

Could a woman be both? Because in Noah's estimation, Bree was.

Pretty as a peach, as Marge had noted. Cute in the way she tried to avoid attention, had a quick-draw temper when coming to someone's defense, and in the way she daintily dipped each french fry in ketchup exactly three times before she ate it.

But after spending just a few days with her, Noah pegged her as being made up of so much more. And he was hooked. Already, he spent way too much time obsessing about learning her likes and dislikes, her past, her dreams—and yes, her secrets, too.

And then there was the growing obsession to have her under him, naked and thrashing with need. He gave a mental shrug. No sense in denying it, especially to himself.

Unfortunately, she was wound tighter than an eight-day clock, and he was stuck trying to figure her out while on the job, bit by arduous bit. Because no matter how intrigued he was by Brianna Delgado, priority one for him was to be taken seriously. To be given cases to work on his own.

So while he might desire the only female deputy in the Boone County Sheriff's Department, dating Bree wouldn't help his cause. Knowing Cassie, probably just the opposite.

As he finished adding Sandy's statement, as well as the pictures she'd emailed, to their report, Bree came to his desk with a printed-out summary of what had happened at the hospital with the young boy.

"I checked in with the nurses' station, and they confirmed he was definitely exposed to toxins related to meth. They don't know the full extent of his internal injuries, but the prognosis isn't good. Apparently, he absorbed a near-lethal amount for someone his size, but he's a fighter. Hanging on by a thread." Bree's face, her whole stance, radiated rage. Might have included some residual anger left over from her confrontation with Dave, but probably not. She was definitely a champion of the underdogs.

Noah, also angry on behalf of the child as well as his mom, swallowed the sudden lump in this throat. "It makes me sick every time I remember his small body on that gurney." He rose, and they headed for Adam's office. "If I were his father, I'd be tempted to find the creeps who dumped that trash and leave *them* lying in the ditch."

Bree nodded. "Too many kids start out life at a disadvantage. And then even ones like this little boy, with loving parents and a decent home, get hurt or kidnapped or fall in with a bad crowd." Somehow, she found a smile. A sad one, but still…a smile. "All we can do is find the bastards who did this and shut them down."

Noah knocked on Adam's door. Six months ago, Adam didn't even have a door. Or an office. He'd sat at the desk in the corner of the bullpen with the rest of the deputies. But stick the word *chief* in front of *deputy*, and the new title came with a door prize.

"Come in." Adam looked up from his computer, his usual serious expression in place. "Heard you two have had quite the day, huh?"

"Yep, and still plenty of it left." Noah pulled out a visitor's chair for Bree before taking the other one. "Report's filed on the Sweets and Treats incident, and the culprit is in our detox cell."

Adam frowned. "We don't have a detox cell."

"We do now." Noah chuckled.

Adam turned his gaze to Bree. "And how's your first week going?"

"Unexpectedly exhilarating." She reached across the desk and handed Adam the summary on the toxic exposure. "This was everything we saw and heard at the hospital, from the moment the boy came in until we left. While we waited for our detainee's blood work, we had ample time to speak with the child's mother."

"And?"

"We have a high degree of confidence that his family has no connection to the drugs or trash. The boy is an only child, his father's a roughneck on a drilling rig off the coast and the mother is a stay-at-home mom. The next-door neighbors, who own the property where the child was playing, are an older couple who attend the same church as our victim's family." Bree paused, started to say something, then closed her mouth.

Adam gave her a warm smile. "Go ahead, Deputy. What's on your mind?"

"It's unusual for meth cookers to dump their toxic trash near their own house, sir, unless they just throw it in the backyard. The usual MO for them is to take a drive somewhere and toss it out the window so it won't be connected to them."

Noah sat back, impressed with Bree's knowledge.

But what really caught his attention was the way she presented the information to Adam: with deference to her superiors, her words succinct—to the point—and not one wisecrack. Bet no one questioned *her* seriousness on the job.

Well, okay then. If he wanted his siblings to see him in the same way, he'd need to take a page from her playbook.

Adam glanced down at the paper he was holding, then back at Bree. "Did you work a lot of drug cases in San Antonio?"

"A fair number, yes, sir. We also had extensive training in dealing with people high on different drugs as well as handling meth-house scenarios." She paused and gulped a breath of air, as if fortifying herself for the rest. "The lingering toxicity inside the building, possibility of explosions—pretty much anything that could happen."

"Sounds like you have more knowledge about meth than our entire department combined. Do me a favor. As soon as you two join the drug investigation, speak to Helen and get on the schedule for the morning briefing." His brother's rarely seen smile flickered to life again. "I'd appreciate it if you'd spend—oh, I don't know—about fifteen or twenty minutes sharing your knowledge with the rest of the department."

A hesitant smile appeared on her face. "Yes, sir. Whatever I can do to help."

"Outstanding." Adam stood. "Our sheriff was right, as usual. You're going to become an excellent addition to our department, and particularly to this investigation, as it seems the case just keeps on getting bigger."

A slow burn crawled through Noah. A petty sensation that he hated but couldn't stop. He hadn't been assigned to the case, even though he was first on the scene. Now Bree, a deputy here for exactly— he glanced at his watch—three days, five hours and twenty minutes was being hailed as the be-all and end-all of the department.

Adam glanced at Noah. "You two will still be riding together until the sheriff returns, and we need to get the high school burglary wrapped up. After that, I'd like you both on the meth case with me."

Shocked by his brother's announcement, then deeply ashamed of his thoughts just moments earlier, Noah maintained a serious expression. While he couldn't bring himself to address Adam as *sir*, he could at least show his brother the proper respect due someone in his position.

Noah stood, biting his tongue against any protests, wisecracks or even one harmless little joke. "We're on it, sir."

Dang if that "sir" didn't just slip on out. And it didn't taste nearly as bitter as he'd expected it would. The faint nod of approval he received from Adam in return made it worth it.

Hell, he'd call Adam *sir* all day long and twice on Sunday for a chance to run his own investigation, as long as Bree was at his side.

Chapter Eight

Bree speed-walked back to the bullpen, relieved when she found Dave Saunders gone. She'd had enough of him today, and she and Noah had a lot to do. Under the best of circumstances, an investigation could be slow, laborious work, but even more so in Resolute. The one thing they'd planned on doing today was the one thing still not done.

Bree checked her watch. "We better get going if we want the list of people who have keys to the high school."

Noah pulled a folded sheet of paper from his back pocket. Wearing a triumphant grin, he held it up. "We don't need to. I stopped by the school on my way back from lunch and picked it up."

"I thought we'd planned to interview anyone still at the school while we were there." Bree struggled to keep her voice free of exasperation.

"That *was* the plan. But then something Bishop said about a case he's working got me thinking. It makes more sense to check the backgrounds of all our suspects before we talk to them."

Infected by Noah's exuberance, Bree's irritation sloughed away. In some ways he was still like a rookie: excited about every discovery, proud of every good idea.

She nodded her approval. "We might catch them in a lie from the get-go."

"Yeah, and less back-and-forth." Noah planted himself at his desk.

She rolled a chair over from another desk and sat next to him. He spread the paper open, and they both leaned over it, almost knocking heads. Before Bree could pull back, Noah turned. They were face-to-face. Noses almost touching. His dark, penetrating eyes locked with hers. The magnetic force captivated her, filling her with a torrent of sensual energy.

Get a grip, girl. Before she made a complete jerk of herself, Bree summoned a Herculean amount of willpower and pulled her gaze from his. An almost impossible task when she inhaled his faint earthy scent of cedar and eucalyptus.

Noah shifted in his chair and cleared his throat.

He's not unaffected, either. That mollified her. Somewhat.

"Okay, this is everyone who was issued a master key to the school." Noah tapped the paper.

Focus on the list of names. "That's a pretty short list."

"According to Principal Jackson, the teachers don't get a master key—just one for their classroom. If they have to get into the school after hours, it's arranged ahead of time for someone to meet them and let them in. In an emergency, either Jackson or a custodian needs to be called to unlock the main door, then walk them back out and lock up behind them."

"So administrators and custodians, then." Still distracted by his close proximity, Bree pushed away from the desk to put some real estate between them.

Noah added to the distance by leaning back in his chair and crossing his arms over his chest. "Well, administration-wise, there's just the principal who has the master key. Then there are the three custodians and the maintenance man. The vice principals and other admin staff don't have master keys. We'll ignore the principal for obvious reasons."

Bree jerked upright in her chair. "Whoa, whoa, whoa. Just because he's been there forever and you respect him, doesn't mean we shouldn't look into him."

"And normally, you'd be absolutely right. But the weekend of the break-in, he and Mrs. Jackson were in Houston, visiting their grandkids." Noah's eyes sparked with humor. "We still need to verify that, of course, but I think it's a safe bet that he's not our guy."

As much as Bree wanted to wipe the smug smile from his face, she found herself amused. And that wasn't her style. What was it about Noah Reed that turned her ordered existence upside down? "You could have led with that."

"Where's the fun in that?" He tapped his finger by the next names on the list. "So that leaves the head custodian, his assistant and the guy who polishes the floors. The floor polisher fills in as needed if one of the first two are out. Plus, the maintenance man."

"I thought you said the teachers don't have keys."

Bree pointed to the last grouping of names. "I clearly see Coach Crawford's name. I'm assuming the rest are the athletic department staff. What gives?" Even Bree didn't miss the acid in her question. Nothing like blatant school favoritism to cool her ardor.

Noah gave her a quick look. He'd noticed her attitude change. "Between nighttime basketball games in the gym, extra innings in baseball and football games on weekends, the coaches need access around the clock. Didn't make sense for them to pay a custodian to be on constant call. We'll take a look at the coaching staff, but I think we should leave them for last."

Bree narrowed her eyes. How many times had she railed against the inequity of it all? "Interesting." Sarcasm dripped from the word. The push and pull between athletics and education was anything *but* interesting. It was shameful. "Less than a thousand kids total at the school, and that department has five coaches. Poor Ben Irving uses bandages and spit to hold on to... What? Thousand-dollar laptops? But the athletic department—"

"Before you completely dog Resolute High's coaching staff, between the five of them, they cover every competitive sport Resolute participates in, either as a head coach or an assistant. Three of them, including Coach Crawford, also teach other subjects like history and math. The other two, in addition to coaching, teach phys ed." Noah's smile had disappeared.

She held up her hands in surrender. "Just forget it."

"I don't get what your problem is with our sports program."

"It's not *Resolute's* program. It's sports programs in general. You know how it is. In bigger school districts, at least in Texas, it's common for a huge slice of the budget to go toward sports. I've seen some high schools that have football-coaching staffs almost as big as NFL teams."

For once, Noah remained silent. Allowing her to make her point? Or too angry to speak? Whatever he was thinking, she needed to soften the rhetoric. "I just think more money should go to academic and outreach programs for under-resourced kids. I'm not saying sports in school aren't important. They are. But equally important is keeping kids who don't participate in sports off the streets and out of trouble. Keeping them busy with community projects. Teaching them how to navigate the parts of life after high school that they don't learn about *in* high school." Bree massaged her forehead. "The schools do as much as they can with the money allocated toward programs like that. But it's usually not enough."

Noah uncrossed his arms and straightened in his chair. "So what's the solution? You're fighting a losing battle in the 'God, family and football' state."

"Believe me, I know. That's why I started a youth program through my precinct in San Antonio." *And this is where I need to shut up.* She closed her eyes, took a deep breath and got herself under control. To protect her secret, she'd sworn to keep to herself at the new job—and here she was, blowing that big time. At this rate, how long before she revealed more than just her personal opinions? "Look, we need to focus on the investigation here. So, the principal's not a suspect. Why leave the coaches for later?"

Like a desperate man, Noah seemed to leap at the change in topics. "Because Crawford reported the break-in. Besides, why steal equipment he has access to all the time? Same for the other coaches. Like I said, we'll check them all out, of course, but—"

"Could they be throwing us off with the sports equipment, while what they really wanted was something from one of the other departments?"

"Possibly. That's one of the angles we need to look at."

"But you like the cleaning crew for this? More than anyone else?"

Noah shook his head. "No, not really. For the same reason. They already have access. Why stage a break-in?" His gaze drifted away from her for a moment. "I've known most of these men for a long time. I know you're going to say I'm biased, but I just don't think they look good for this. However, we'll still start with them."

"Do you have the final inventory list yet?" Bree asked, satisfied with Noah's game plan.

Noah scrolled through his work emails. "Yeah. Here it is. I'm forwarding it to you."

Leaving the borrowed chair at Noah's desk, Bree crossed over to the far corner and logged in to her work computer. "Okay, I've got it."

Bree scrolled through the inventory, comparing it to the preliminary list they'd received earlier from the principal. The list of missing sports equipment hadn't changed, and still nothing was missing from the computer lab. From the science department, the list of missing or broken items had become longer and more detailed. The number of beakers and funnels, stirring rods and petri dishes was updated. Boxes of slides, a drying oven, Bunsen burners and two microscopes. As the science teacher had said, no rhyme or reason.

Bree returned to the empty chair next to Noah. "Okay, it makes sense that the coaches wouldn't have attempted to steal anything from the computer lab, since they all have their own work computers." To be absolutely sure, they'd confirmed that with Coach Crawford on Monday.

Noah nodded. "Even if one of the coaching staff wanted a laptop not issued by the school, to watch porn or access the dark web, it would've been easier to just pick up a cheap or used one somewhere."

"We also have to consider that a key could have been swiped and copied, then the original returned. Or someone on the list could have lost theirs and borrowed someone else's to make a copy without reporting it." From her back pocket, Bree pulled out a small notebook and began writing.

The list of names. The list of missing items. Leads to follow. Her personal impressions. Anything she could think of, because sometimes when there were a million facts to consider, you forgot the details.

A quick glance in Noah's direction showed that he was making notes, too, but on his computer. Her mouth twitched as she noted how old-school she was when building a case compared to him. And then she

noted other things about him. How he tapped one finger against his lips while he stared at his monitor. How his fingers flew over the keys when he typed. How—
Stop it. Stay focused.

Her mind churned. Not to mention her libido. "Let's split the list. I'll find out what I can on the head custodian and his assistant. You can have the other two."

Without looking up, Noah nodded.

Bree started with the head custodian, Bill "Rusty" Nails.

Bree snorted. Rusty Nails? Poor guy. *Bet he was teased to no end when he was a kid.* She opened the background-check program.

Along with the list of names, Principal Jackson had also sent basic employee information. Based on his picture, fifty-six-year-old Rusty had no doubt acquired his nickname due to his full head of reddish-orange hair. He'd worked at Resolute High for almost forty years, ever since he'd graduated from the school himself. Married, he and his wife had three children who were now out-of-the-house married adults with kids themselves. No police record for him, not so much as a parking ticket.

Jack Williams, the assistant custodian, was a different story. Twenty-six years old and single, he'd worked with Nails for the last seven years. His juvenile record was sealed, but the fact that he had one meant nothing good. One, two—no, *four*—public-intoxication arrests and a handful of drunk-and-disorderly charges since turning twenty-one, the latest just a few months ago. One of these involved misdemeanor-assault charges.

A real charmer. Definitely someone who might run afoul of the law for more than just swilling his booze and getting physical. She put a star next to his name and looked up from her computer. "You familiar with this guy, Jack Williams?"

"We've hauled him in a time or two. Not the sharpest crayon in the box—and I'm talking the big box, 152 colors and a sharpener." Noah spread his arms wide to exaggerate the box size. "By the time he starts getting into fights, he's usually so drunk he just swings and follows his fist around into a cowboy pirouette."

"What on earth is a 'cowboy pirouette'?"

"Like the kind in ballet, except the guy is drunk as a skunk, misses his target and his momentum carries him around and down. Oh, and he's wearing jeans and boots instead of tights and those shoes that make you stand on your toes."

"You mean pointe shoes?"

Noah's eyes widened in surprise. "*You* know what they're called?"

"What? You think a cop can't like things like the ballet or opera?"

Noah's face screwed up. "You like *opera*?"

"Hell no." Bree laughed. "But I do enjoy the ballet."

"Good luck with that in Resolute." Noah stretched his arms above his head. "You ready? I've got enough on the maintenance man and the night guy who does floors to start with."

Bree glanced at her watch. "I'm ready, but it's three forty-five, and school will be letting out around now.

It'll be hard to talk to any of them privately. Besides, we might learn more if they let us into their homes."

"Works for me." Noah yawned. "I need a little downtime. Meet you in the parking lot at six?"

"See you then."

He gathered up his personal belongings and headed out. For half a minute, while he was still in sight, Bree allowed herself to enjoy the view. Handsome face, dreamy eyes, ripped physique—not to mention a winning smile. Throw in an offbeat sense of humor and his enjoyment of the smallest things in life, and Bree knew she was in trouble.

Get out of my head, Noah Reed. But he was like a tick that had burrowed under her skin.

In the past, whenever Bree had found herself on an emotional roller coaster, she could always fall back on the job. The job was her saving grace. The job was everything. Heck, the job was the reason she was here. For all that Noah called to her on so many levels, it was well past time she remembered that protecting her job would always be the most important thing to her.

And to do that, keeping things professional with Noah and laying low in general were imperative. Now Adam's voice popped into her head, asking her to speak at a morning briefing about drugs.

Stellar job you're doing of keeping off everyone's radar, Bree.

She pulled up the reports that Noah had run on the maintenance man and the third custodian. Both were older men. Both had been with the Boone County School District for decades and at Resolute High for at least fifteen years. She printed out everything on all four men and went to the break room. Opening the fridge, she retrieved the half sandwich she'd saved from lunch, grabbed a can of Diet Coke from the vending machine and began rereading everything.

After all, forewarned was forearmed. Especially since she couldn't trust herself to pull her actual firearm. *Yet.*

NOAH PARKED IN front of the justice center's steps at 6:00 p.m. on the dot. The last streaks of an orange-and-purple sky disappeared below the western horizon, and he was pleased to find Bree already waiting. He believed in punctuality, one of the few characteristics he shared with his big sister.

Bree's dark blue Ford F-150, an older model, sat in the next space with its windows fogged over. She locked the vehicle and slid into his passenger seat, bringing with her a blast of icy air unusual for the area, even in January. A chill raced through Noah, and he cranked up the heat.

Bree adjusted the collar on her heavy jacket before buckling herself in. "Am I imagining things, or is it colder this winter?"

"Seems every winter's colder than the last one." Noah backed out of the parking space and headed east, past downtown businesses and historic homes. "Rusty Nails first?"

"That name," Bree said, a smile behind the words. "Sure, why not? Seems best to begin at the top, especially since you think he's a long shot to be our guy.

Would be great to start crossing names off the list."
She flipped open the file folder on her lap. "I brought a
printout of our background checks on everyone. Rusty
lives on Baker Street."

"Whoa, Delgado, you didn't have to kill a tree. We
can always pull it up again on here." Noah laughed, determined to keep things light as he tapped the computer
in his department vehicle. Despite the obvious heat that
existed between them, their relationship needed to stay
strictly professional if he wanted to impress Cassie and
change his reputation in the department. "You do have
mobile-data terminals in San Antonio, don't you?"

"Ha ha ha. Yes, we have MDTs. It's just that I ab-
sorb more when I read a hard copy." She waved the
thin folder at him. "Besides, it would've been a pretty
small sapling if this tiny stack killed it."

He'd been admiring her attention to detail since her
first day on the job. Her head always on a swivel, taking in everything. Asking questions if she didn't already know the answer, getting confirmation if she
did. And apparently, she didn't just read their investigative reports and background checks—she *studied*
them. Her career path seemed to point toward a detective in the making. Which made her decision to come
to Resolute all the more curious.

They came to a neighborhood of modest clapboard
houses with yards of winter-brown grass and bare trees,
except for the live oaks. The sidewalks were empty,
no doubt the frigid air and thoughts of dinner driving people inside. "What's the house number?" Noah
glanced across the console at Bree.

Her profile leaned more toward cute than pretty, with her pert nose and short, loose curls going every which way. "2725 Baker." She hadn't referred to her file; she'd already memorized it.

He parked in front of the Nailses' home and switched off the engine.

Bree turned to him. "Ready?"

Her blue eyes sparkled, most likely with the thrill of the hunt. Definitely not from some burning desire for him. Oh, he was no idiot. She was attracted to him on the surface, but it didn't go any further than that. Instead of appreciating humor in the day-to-day, she was dead serious about pretty much everything, especially her career. As he should be.

Deputy Brianna Delgado might help him solve cases and prove himself worthy on the job. But *Bree* was a powerful distraction who teased and enticed him, like the glint off a fishing lure hiding sharp, dangerous hooks.

He took a deep breath. "Ready." And he was.

Chapter Nine

Thank goodness for the frosty air outside. Bree, burning up from sitting so close to Noah, sucked in deep breaths of it. Just when it seemed she had her overactive libido in check, he gave her a look or a smile that shot her control to smithereens. And the explosive aftermath left her happy, optimistic and grinning like a fool for no obvious reason.

This reaction to a man had never happened to her before, and it bothered her to no end. The return of the sheriff and the end of her partnering with Noah couldn't happen soon enough for her peace of mind.

"Good grief. Come on in out of the cold." Rusty held his front door open. He didn't seem surprised by their unannounced visit. Or he was just the type who enjoyed drop-in guests.

Her frozen cheeks tingled when she walked into the Nailses' overheated home. The small, cozy living room was immaculate, the only exception a pile of crocheted something-or-other on one corner of the couch, its dangling yarn leading to a basket of multicolored skeins. An inviting, easy place that reminded Bree of her beloved grandmother. Yet another unexpected tug on her emotional heartstrings.

I'm a mess.

"Take off your coats and sit a spell." Rusty waved at the other end of the couch as he took the well-used recliner and muted the news program he'd been watching. The hair responsible for his moniker was more white than red these days. What was left of it, anyway. Lean and well-groomed, he wore nice slacks and a heavy plaid flannel shirt.

Bree and Noah removed their jackets and hung them on the coatrack near the front door as Rusty hollered, "Iris? Come on out here and offer these deputies something to warm their bellies." He chuckled. "I don't know about you folks, but my bones don't take to the cold so much these days."

Mrs. Nails hustled into the living room from the kitchen, wiping her hands on a dish towel. "Gracious. You two look frozen stiff. I was just washing up the dinner dishes, but let me get some coffee on. Or perhaps you'd like hot tea?" Her appearance was opposite that of her husband's in almost every way. Tiny, round and with a darkish stain down the front of her blouse, she seemed as friendly as her affable spouse.

"Coffee would be great." Noah sat on the empty end of the couch.

"Let me help." Bree followed the woman into a tidy kitchen. Dinner dishes sat in the drying rack on the Formica countertop. A row of small plants lined the sill of a window over the sink. Like the front room, it was cozy without being cluttered, an easy thing to happen in a small home. Bree ought to know. Her mother had been a borderline hoarder, and to this day, Bree detested clutter.

Besides discovering the Nails were neatniks, Bree found that everything in their home was comfortably worn. No new purchases, no apparent ill-gotten gains from a burglary windfall. Bree also noticed nothing that would indicate a love of science, so no need to steal petri dishes and Bunsen burners. No sports equipment tagged with Resolute High's name, either. Not that any of that would be sitting out in plain sight if they *did* have it. But Noah's assessment that Rusty was not their perp seemed to be on target.

Mrs. Nails loaded the coffee maker, pulled out two mugs and then planted her backside against the counter while they waited for the coffee to brew. "What's your name, dear?"

"Bree."

"Well, Bree, you didn't need to help me, but I really do appreciate the company." She pointed to the living room, where her husband was head-to-head with Noah, reminiscing about the days when Noah ran the hallways as a student. "The old coot watches the news every night at this time and then again at ten, as if something monumental will pop up in the few hours between broadcasts. The man is like clockwork. In fact, I'd venture to say he hasn't missed a newscast in over twenty years. If not for my crocheting, I think I might have lost my mind ages ago." She leveled the criticism with a smile and obvious affection.

Bree said nothing. It had been her experience that

people revealed all types of things when given a receptive audience and free rein. Mrs. Nails went on blathering away, either unaware or unconcerned that her husband was a potential person of interest in the school break-in.

"So, Bree, you must be the new deputy brought in to fill the opening. I suppose you heard all about the ambush of the former sheriff." She gave Noah a sympathetic look. "Noah's father. So sad. Wallace Reed was such a wonderful man. Practically raised those kids on his own after their mother up and disappeared without a word. Just a tragic death. I don't think a single one of them has come to terms with his loss yet."

Whoa. Bree had heard about the former sheriff being killed in the line of duty. And of course, the last name tied him to half the department. But no one ever mentioned him, and she'd failed to regard the deceased man as a father they still grieved. She'd just learned more about the Reed family in three minutes with Mrs. Nails than in almost a week of working with Noah.

So, I'm not the only one with demons haunting my past.

When the coffee was done, Mrs. Nails loaded the mugs, along with cream and sugar, onto a tray and returned to the living room with Bree in tow. She handed Noah a mug, then one to Bree. "Help yourself to the coffee fixings." She sat opposite Noah on the far end of the couch and picked up her crocheting.

Noah, Bree had noted, drank his coffee black. She added in some cream to hers, glad Marge of the Busy B wasn't around to insist she add sugar. *Ah, this was heaven.* The coffee was hot, smooth and pleasantly bitter on her tongue. Choosing an accent chair, Bree sat and placed her mug on the side-table coaster, then pulled out her notebook and pen to take notes.

"Well, let's get on with the reason you're here," Mr. Nails insisted once they'd had time enough for several warming sips.

From joking and laughing, Noah went into serious mode, which he seemed able to do at the drop of a hat. "You know about the break-in at the high school, right?" He took another sip of his coffee, then found a place to rest his mug.

"'Course I know about the break-in. Had to get the window replaced in the gym door." The custodian shook his head. "Like those darn kids don't make enough work for us already."

"What makes you think it was kids?" Noah crossed one ankle over the opposite knee in a relaxed pose. It was a casual move, probably a habit, but the way his thigh muscles bunched almost made her mouth water. How in tarnation did he manage to pull off that degree of sexy with absolutely no effort whatsoever? *So* aggravating. "Have you heard anything about who it might have been?"

"No one's talking about it, but who else could it be but kids? Probably figured the mess would be enough to get them a day off of school." He huffed. "You got any leads?"

"Nothing substantial. We wanted to get your opinion about something." Noah sipped more coffee. "Any chance someone could have gotten hold of a key to the school, used it to get in?"

A frown creased Rusty's forehead, and he took his time before answering. "Well, now that you mention it, there was something hinky about the way that door looked. Can't quite put my finger on it." His expression cleared. "Besides, if someone already had a key, why not use it instead of *breaking* in?"

"That's what we're trying to figure out." He uncrossed his leg and leaned toward Rusty. "You think there's a chance any of your crew lost their key? Or loaned a copy to someone?"

The custodian's face turned as red as his hair must have been once upon a time. "Are you accusing—"

"No, I'm not accusing anyone of anything." Noah held up his hands in a calm-down gesture. "We have to explore every possibility, rule out everyone we can in order to narrow our list of suspects."

After a tense moment, Rusty gave a sharp nod. "Fair enough. You've got a job to do, same as everyone else. But I vouch for my men."

Noah and Rusty stood, and the two women followed suit. Mrs. Nails had kept her nose buried in her crocheting the entire time, but her hook flew through those stitches at top speed when her husband's voice rose. They moved to the front door as a foursome, everyone smiling and the two men shaking hands.

"I'd like to ask a favor, Rusty." Noah handed Bree her jacket and shrugged into his own. "Please don't mention our talk to anyone at the school. Not even your own crew."

Rusty waved his hand. "Don't worry—mum's the word. Right, Iris?" He gave his wife a stern eye, apparently trying to nip gossip in the bud.

She rolled her eyes. "My lips are sealed."

As Noah opened the front door, Bree leaned toward Iris. "I love your needlework. I've never had a knack for it, but I know the skill and patience it takes."

"Oh, thank you, dear. So nice of you to say. I'd be happy to teach you, if you have the time and inclination. It's much easier than it looks." The older woman patted Bree's arm. "Feel free to stop over anytime. I'd love the company."

Bree thanked her as she left, stopping just short of committing to crochet lessons. But she didn't completely rule it out. For however long it took her to work through her hesitation about drawing her piece, she'd need something to occupy her free time. Crocheting was as good as anything. Something to remind her of her grandmother. Something she could do alone.

After the warmth of the Nailses' home, the outside cold was especially brutal. Bree pulled up the collar on her jacket. Noah rubbed his hands together for warmth as they jogged to the SUV. "You did good in there."

As she opened the passenger-side door, Bree shot him a look that said he better tread carefully. "What do you mean?"

Noah climbed in. "I mean, I believe you've just gone forty or so minutes without making anyone mad."

Bree slammed her door shut and reached over to turn on the heater—not that it would do any good until the engine warmed up. "Give me a sec. I'm sure I can change that in no time."

"Hot to cold, cold to hot. Hell of a skill set you've got there, Delgado."

You have no idea, Reed. No idea at all.

WHILE WAITING FOR the SUV to warm up, Noah lifted the file folder from Bree's lap and flipped it open. "We can catch the janitor who polishes the floors later, at the school, since he works nights. Let's save him for last." He rifled through the papers. "Maintenance guy or assistant custodian next?"

"The maintenance man has been working there almost as long as Rusty. Seems odd that one of the long-timers would suddenly do something like this." She leaned across the console and scanned the paper in Noah's hand. "I vote we talk to Ed Charleston, head of maintenance."

She tipped her head to meet his eyes, her curls releasing a scent that brought images of palm trees and beaches. Coconut. Citrus. A tropical flower he could picture but had no name for. Her lips, close enough to kiss, parted slightly. He just needed to lean in a fraction of an inch—

In one swift move, Bree straightened and was back on her side of the console as if nothing had almost happened. Noah released a silent sigh of frustration. With any luck, his sister would decide Bree was ready to solo sooner than later. Then he'd be rid of the constant temptation that tortured him when he was with her. Not just her physical attraction but a bone-deep hankering to know everything about her.

He glanced at Ed's address, handed the file back to Bree and pulled away from the curb. Just a few blocks away from the Nailses' residence, Noah parked in front of another older home. This entire neighborhood featured small houses with neat yards.

Bree, silent during the short drive, paused with her fingers on the door handle. "Want to do the talking again?"

"Sure. But when we visit Jack Williams after Ed, I think we should both question him. I've arrested him several times and he doesn't know you, so double-teaming him might knock him off balance."

He could tell by how her lips tried to twitch into a smile that Bree liked this plan.

They climbed out and started up the walk. Before Noah could ring the bell, a porch light came on and the front door opened.

A large, square man stood in the entry, wearing a belligerent frown. "Wondered how long before you got around to asking us questions. Might as well come in." Ed Charleston stepped back and held the door for them.

"'Us'?" Noah asked, and by the rise of her brow, he knew Bree's curiosity was also piqued.

"*Us*, as in maintenance-and-cleaning crew. If anything goes missing or gets broken, it's always us who get blamed."

Once they were inside, out of the cold, Noah shook Ed's hand. "We're not just interviewing the cleaning and maintenance employees."

"Came to us first, though, didn't you?" Although his hostility was evident, he was keeping it in check. But if this man had any information, Noah doubted he'd be sharing it.

Bree suddenly leaned forward, a ridiculous, toothy grin on her face. "Hi there. I'm Deputy Delgado. My partner has absolutely no manners—but then, Marge over at the Busy B warned me about that. Do you know Marge?"

Ed laughed, a bit strained, but a laugh. "Everybody knows Marge. Here, let me take your jacket."

"Thanks, Mr. Charleston."

"Since we're about to talk all personal-like, call me Ed."

She gave the man a warm smile. "So, Ed, you were expecting us?"

Leading the way into a living room that smelled of cooked cabbage and spicy sausage, Ed motioned for them to sit on the couch. "It only makes sense you'd be talking to people at the school, employees and students. And like I said, we're usually first." He ran a weathered hand across his gray-stubbled chin. "Though that whole break-in is a mite curious, if you ask me."

"How so?" Noah welcomed new thoughts about the case.

"Looked amateur. Which would lead you to think it was a kid, or kids." He tapped a calloused finger against his chin. "Seems to me that kids would only be interested in gym equipment, once they found out that Irving's computers weren't worth the effort." He chuckled. "Gotta hand it to old Ben. But I had to ask myself, if it was kids, why mess with the other departments? Could've just been random vandalism, I suppose, like kids sometimes get up to. But then I got to wondering—where were the dirty words in spray paint? The empty beer cans? You know, things like that? Unless…"

"Yes?" Bree prompted after a few seconds of silence.

Always pushing, Noah noted. She never just let the information flow. Not always a bad thing. Not always a good thing, either.

"Well, unless they were trying to mislead you. You know, trying to cover up something else. Can't figure out what that would be, mind you, but I was wondering."

"That's one possibility we're considering," Noah said. "You think there's any chance someone got their hands on one of the school keys?" He stopped short of suggesting ways it might have happened, curious to see what Ed might come up with.

The older man settled against the back of his chair and gave Noah a shrewd look. "Clued in on that, did you? No one could have come in that gym door without the bottom lock being unlocked."

Noah nodded. "Yep, we caught that right away." He ignored Bree's smirk at the word *we*.

"Well, I can't speak for anyone else, but I have possession of my key to the school. You're welcome to compare my fingerprints to any at the crime scene—but since me and the custodians touch just about every surface in the place on the regular, not sure it'll help." As he spoke, he dug out a key ring from his pocket. He unclipped the chain it was attached to from his belt, sorted through the many keys and passed the ring to Bree, sitting closest to him.

She took it by the key he'd been holding, examined it closely and then passed it to Noah.

It was similar to most keys he'd seen, other than the etched warning not to duplicate. "If one of these did get lost, whoever found it wouldn't have a clue as to what it opened. But I doubt you misplace *your* keys very often." Noah held up the chain. "I don't know how you relax at home with all this still attached to your pants."

"After a while, you get so used to it, you feel naked with it off." Ed chuckled. "'Less of course, you *are* naked."

Chuckling along with Ed, Bree asked, "Do you have any thoughts on who might've broken in?"

If he was a betting man—and he was—Noah would have placed money on Bree getting offended by this joke. And he would've lost. This easygoing demeanor of hers was a far cry from her usual approach, but it, as well as her keen powers of observation, could only help solve the case. Even if the extent of her flirtatious behavior rankled him a bit.

Ed shook his head. "I do have thoughts on who *wouldn't* have. For us older guys—Rusty, Bud and me—if we wanted something enough to steal it, we'd just slip it out of the school with our tools or in a bucket or something. Now, I'm not saying we'd actually do that. I'm just saying none of us got the energy to go about it like a burglary. We spend our weekends drinkin' beer, watchin' football and restin' up for the following week."

"You didn't include Jack Williams in that group." Noah kept a sharp eye on Ed's expression.

"Well, now, Jack's a mite younger, and I don't know him very well." He paused as if considering how to explain further. "Hasn't been at the high school long. I'd hate to think Rusty's pup had anything to do with it, but I can't vouch for him like I can Rusty and Bud."

Bree pulled her brows together in a look of confusion. "'Pup'?"

"His assistant." Ed snickered. "That kid follows him around like a puppy from the pound. Has since they hired him. If he don't start takin' on some responsibilities, I doubt he's long for the scintillating world of janitorial work."

Bree snorted, then tried to cover it up with a cough.

Ed pretended to be offended. "I'll have you know I learn a new word every day, young lady. I just open the dictionary, close my eyes and point. *Scintillating* happened to be yesterday's word." His lips fought to contain a smile; then he and Bree gave in to laughter.

As it tapered off, Ed wiped his eyes. "Whoo-ee! I can't remember the last time I had a good laugh with a pretty lady. Y'all need to come question me more often."

Instead of taking his head off for calling her a lady, like she nearly had Dave's, Bree smiled. "Aren't you sweet."

Her tone was still syrupy enough to cause a toothache, and Noah rose, shaking his head at both of them.

"Well, I may not be the pretty one, but maybe we can all just meet up for beers instead."

Standing, Ed shook his hand. "Got yourself a deal, Noah." He turned to shake Bree's as she joined the men. "And by the way, Deputy Delgado, welcome to Resolute."

"Thank you, Mr.—"

The older man held up a finger as if to scold her. "I told you to forget that *mister* nonsense."

"Thank you, Ed. And I'm Bree."

Noah handed him a card. "If you think of anything else or hear something, give me a call, okay?"

"Will do." The man pocketed the card, his keys jangling as he did so. "And after you two solve this case, call me for that beer."

"You're on." Noah handed Bree's jacket to her and put on his own. Once they were outside, she gave him a questioning look. He waited until they were back in the car.

"He seems nice." Her pleasant expression from a moment ago had faded into one of concentration. "But you know him better than I do." She shivered and wrapped her arms around her body. "What do you think?"

"What he said made a lot of sense." Noah glanced at the dash clock. "We still have time to talk to Williams—and at this point, he sounds like our most interesting person of interest." He grinned.

"Seriously? Is that what passes for wit these days?" Slightly miffed that he didn't garner the same reaction that Ed had from his jokes, Noah cranked up the heater. "You're just jealous you didn't say it first."

Bree scoffed. "As if." She dropped her head back against the seat. "And speaking of jealousy, what the heck was your deal in there?"

"*My* deal?" Noah buckled his seat belt.

Bree snapped hers in place as well. "Half the time I was talking to him, you were either rolling your eyes or glaring at me."

Noah batted his eyelashes; then, in a breathy falsetto voice, he said, "Hi there, Ed, you big old cutie pie. I'm Bree. Blink, blink, blink. Why, you are so terribly funny. Blink, blink, blink." He ended with a high-pitched giggle.

Bree's mouth hung open. "You were antagonizing him to the point that I thought he'd kick us out. Stop sounding like a jealous boyfriend. I was simply getting information in a different way."

A jealous *boyfriend*? Not in this lifetime. Plus, he'd never had a jealous bone in his body. "Just didn't think you had it in you to be so phony."

"Lots of things you don't know about me." Bree snapped her mouth shut and went all starch and vinegar. She stretched out her arm and tapped a finger against her watch. "Let's go. Time's a-wastin'."

Aaand she was back. The woman he'd already grown used to. The one he liked as a colleague. *Just* as a colleague. *The fool doth protest too much, methinks.*

Leave it to his brain to misquote Shakespeare.

Chapter Ten

It didn't surprise Bree when Noah pulled into the parking lot of the Oak View Apartments, a place where she'd considered renting. Jack Williams was an assistant custodian in a rural county school district with a tight budget. Unless he wanted to live with his parents, an apartment here might be all he could afford.

On the wall outside the main door to the building, a list of names identified the buzzer for each apartment. Bree grabbed Noah's arm to stop him from pushing Williams's bell.

"Let's try this first." She pushed the buzzer labeled Manager. Instead of asking who it was through the intercom, the door release clicked, and Bree grabbed the handle. "This way, we don't risk Williams leaving by the back door." She entered the tiny foyer and started up the stairs.

"How'd you know there was a back door?" Noah followed on her heels, making her self-conscious of his view.

"At one time, I thought I might rent here." She reached the first landing and continued up the next set of stairs. "Until I saw the vacant apartment. Pretty small and kind of gross."

"Yeah, that could change your mind."

Reaching the top floor, Bree started down the hallway, checking apartment numbers as she went. When they reached Williams's, she motioned for Noah to stand to the side. Music blasted from inside. Scrunching down a little so only her face would show in the peephole, she knocked.

Footsteps approached, then retreated. The music disappeared and a moment later, the door opened, with Williams leaning forward with a black eye and a crooked smile. The smile only lasted a second, until he eyed her badge. "Oh hell, no!" Scrambling backward, he tried to slam the door.

Bree had often been called petite, but her feet never had. She considered them a welcome counterbalance to her also-not-petite boobage. She blocked the door with one foot, and Noah helped her push it open.

"You're hurting my feelings, Jack. Makes me think you're not happy to see me." Noah paused at the threshold, Bree next to him. "Now, we can talk to you from here, if that's what you'd prefer." He leaned back and looked down the hall in both directions, then faced Jack again. "'Course, we'll probably cover more topics than we'd planned on. I sure hope none of your neighbors gets the wrong idea about the extent to which you're helping us on a very important case."

"Come on, man. I haven't done anything." His swollen eye, the only thing marring his handsome face, said otherwise. He threw his arms up in the air. "Fine. Come in."

Noah walked in. "That wasn't so hard, was it?"

Bree closed the door and leaned against it. "How'd you get the shiner?"

Jack gave Noah a sideways glance. "Hit myself in the face with my mop at work."

"I'd admire you for wanting to look stupid instead of guilty, *if* I bought that." Noah sat on what looked like a thrift-store couch and waved toward the mismatched chair. "Have a seat. We just want to ask you a few questions."

"Said every cop who ever arrested me." Jack dropped into the chair.

"Well, yeah, since I'm the cop who usually arrests you." Noah shrugged. "What can I say? Habits are hard to break."

Bree walked over to the only other chair, a wooden one at a small table. "Where were you Friday night?"

Raking both hands through his dark hair, he said, "I swear I didn't get in a fight."

"Not what I asked you." Bree turned the chair around and sat backward on it. For some reason, it bothered men when she did that. Made them more defensive.

"I was at the Dead End until it closed. Playing pool."

Bree gave Noah a questioning glance.

"It's a bar." Then to Jack: "After that?"

"I was here. Sleeping it off." Jack scowled at them. "And again, I didn't get in a fight."

"Were you with anyone?" Bree already had her pad

and pen in her hand. When Jack nodded, she said, "We're gonna need her name. Or his."

He started to rise, so she raised her hands. "Hey. No judgment here."

"It was a woman. And I'm not telling you her name." He blew out a sigh. "She's married, and her husband will kill me if he finds out."

"For a second there, I thought you were protecting her honor." Bree blew out a heavy sigh of her own. "Why don't we cut to the chase. Give us the play-by-play of your whole weekend, from leaving work on Friday to back at work Monday morning."

Jack flopped back in his chair and began a boring, detailed description of his every move during the sixty hours in question. She and Noah listened until the end without interrupting.

"I was wrong, Deputy Delgado." Noah yawned. "Apparently, our most interesting person of interest isn't interesting after all."

"Only if we're expected to believe that a good-looking, charismatic man like Mr. Williams has such a limited social life." Bree winked at Noah.

But he obviously didn't appreciate her attempt to provoke Jack. Instead, Noah's mouth compressed into a hard line, and the skin around his eyes tightened.

What was his problem? He was the one who'd suggested she help throw Williams off balance. Between this and accusing her of being a flirt earlier...did he honestly think she was flirting *now*?

The room had been silent for less than a minute, but it seemed much longer to Bree. She met Jack's eyes.

"I'm sure you heard about the recent break-in at the high school."

"That's what this is about?" He jumped to his feet. "I had nothing to do with that."

"Then who did you loan your school key to?" Noah stood and assumed a challenging pose.

"I don't loan my key to anyone. It's not allowed." Jack's face turned red.

In what? Anger, indignation or frustration at being caught?

"So all of a sudden, you're a rule follower?" Noah asked.

"When it comes to my job, you're damn right. I need that job."

"You have quite the history of shoplifting." Bree rose from her chair as she sensed the conversation coming to a close. "It's not that far-fetched to think you've graduated to burglary."

"How did you know that? Those files were sealed."

"They still are." She stepped closer to Jack. "But you just told me. Oldest trick in the book, and they still fall for it every time."

Noah stepped between them. "How 'bout you let us search your apartment while we're here. As an act of good faith since you say you don't have any of the stolen items."

"How 'bout you come back with a warrant?" Jack's hands squeezed into fists. "Now get out."

Noah held his hands in front of him. "Okay, okay. We're leaving—but know if we have to come back with a warrant, we're going to be *very* thorough."

"Take your best shot."

"Don't be stupid and try to move anything out of your apartment. Someone will be watching you until we come back."

"Get *out*!"

The door slammed behind them with finality. But final only for now. She'd be back, with Noah in tow, and Jack better hope they didn't turn up anything. She never had liked wasting her time.

Noah walked behind her in the narrow hallway. "Based on the interviews, our buddy Jack looks the most promising so far. Everyone else has been cooperating."

"Unless one of the other guys was lying. And we can't forget the coaching staff. Still need to work up backgrounds on them." She glanced over her shoulder and stopped Noah when he opened his mouth to speak. "Look, I know they're a lower priority. But I'm a check-off-all-the-boxes kinda girl."

"I promise we'll get to everyone on the list." He aimed a mischievous smile her way. "But while we're on the subject of Jack, I'm pretty sure you're mistaken about who the good-looking, charismatic one was in there."

Ah, there it was. He'd thought she was flirting and got his man feelings hurt. At least he approached the subject with humor now. Bree turned around and walked backward down the hall, peering at Noah with her head tipped to the side. "Hmm. I suppose it might've been the bad lighting."

"I'm proud of you, Delgado. Takes a big person to admit when they're wrong."

Bree groaned with frustration, then faced forward again before reaching the stairs. Noah *was* the best-looking, most charismatic man she'd met in a long time.

But she wasn't about to let *him* know that.

"You're so full of it," she tossed over her shoulder.

"If you mean full of charm, charisma and a boat-load of magnetism, then yes I am."

"You just go ahead and think whatever makes you feel better about yourself, Reed."

"Always do, Delgado. Always do."

NOAH PULLED INTO the Resolute High parking lot closest to the gym and checked his watch. "It's seven forty-five, on the dot."

"What's going on at this hour?" Bree looked around at the half-full lot and brightly lit building.

"Coach always runs late practice sessions the night before varsity basketball games."

When they approached the door, a young assistant basketball coach unlocked it and let them in.

"Evening, Noah. Ma'am."

"Hi, Isaac. This is Deputy Delgado."

"My pleasure, ma'am. Principal Jackson said you'd be stopping by. I'd almost given up on you."

"Had a few other stops to make first." Noah checked out the court, where the team ran drills. "How much longer will you be here?"

"At least half an hour. Maybe longer." He led the way along the perimeter of the room to the corridor door leading to the main building. Unlocking it, he pushed it open and held it for them to pass through. "Think you'll need more time than that?"

"Half an hour should be plenty. But just in case, can we borrow your key to let ourselves out? I can get it back to you first thing in the morning."

Isaac paused and, as if making a life-altering decision, gazed at Noah's badge while his fingers twirled the key. When he finally made eye contact, he shrugged. "I'm sorry, I can't do that, even if you *are* the law. Especially since the break-in."

"Good answer." Noah clapped him on the shoulder. "You hear about anyone else with a key loaning it out?"

"Or maybe losing theirs?" Bree joined the conversation.

The man shook his head. "We all have to be able to open up and lock up, just in case. If someone lost their key, they'd have to get another one from Coach. And he likes to announce it when people screw up. You know, kinda like a drill sergeant who embarrasses his men in front of the whole platoon?"

Bree was scribbling in her notebook. Without even looking up, she asked, "Couldn't they just have a duplicate made?"

"Nope. The school keys are restricted." The assistant coach smiled. "And I know this for a fact. When I first started here, I was so terrified of losing mine, I tried to get a copy made. The local places wouldn't touch it, so I drove all the way to a locksmith in Victoria. They took one look at it and refused, too."

"So what happens when someone does lose a key?"

Bree stood ready to take more notes, pen tip touching paper.

"A request is sent to the school district, and they order a new one from the manufacturer. A serial number is on each key, and they keep records of who's assigned each one." Isaac scrunched up his face in thought. "As far as loaning a key to someone, I haven't heard anything."

"Gotcha," Noah said. "See you here in about thirty minutes."

"Me and my key will be waiting."

The door clicked closed behind them, and the bolt lock slid into place. Noah and Bree moved at a fast pace down the hallway and into the main building. As they turned a corner, heading deeper into the school, their boot heels thumped out a rhythm on the linoleum floors until challenged by the hum of a floor scrubber. Noah stuck his arm out to the side to stop Bree. "Hear that?"

"I think it's coming from that way." She pointed ahead and to the left, leading him through the hallways.

Three minutes passed, then four. No floor scrubber. Noah could still hear the darn machine humming, so where the heck was the man pushing it around? He picked up the pace and zipped past Bree. "Hurry up, slowpoke. We're losing time, and I don't want to get locked in here."

"Slow down, will you? It's been a long day, and I'm too tired to keep running after you. If we do get locked in, you have Coach Crawford's number. You can just call him."

He hated it when anyone thought of something that

he should have. But with Bree, it sat differently on him. He would have to prove his worth to his siblings, but with her—well, he just wanted her to *know* he was on the ball.

"Hopefully, we'll finish up in no time, so it won't matter." Noah looked over his shoulder to find Bree gaining on him. "If we can just find our guy."

They reached the end of another hallway, rounded another corner and there he was: the janitor, swinging the floor buffer from side to side as he worked his way toward them. But when he glanced up, instead of the older man Noah knew, a young guy—late teens, early twenties—stared at him. Maybe five foot ten and skinny as a rail, he wore ripped jeans and a Rolling Stones classic tongue T-shirt, a hoodie and sneakers. No mistaking him for Bud.

For a split second, the kid's eyes darted back and forth as if debating what to do. Noah instantly pegged him as a runner. And sure enough, he ditched the machine and blazed a path down a side hall. Taking off after him, Noah saw a blur from the corner of his eye. He glanced that direction only to find Bree leaving him in her dust.

She must've gotten a second wind, 'cause that girl could flat out run. He sped up, determined to pass her, but she managed at least two strides to each of his longer ones. She finally slid to a stop at a hallway intersection, breathing hard and waving her hands.

"I'm lost. And I can't hear him running anymore." Bree stomped her foot. "I could've caught him, but this school is a doggone maze."

"Let's try to catch him outside." Noah motioned for her to follow him, and he raced back to the gym. Pounding on the door for it to be unlocked, he cursed the seconds ticking away.

"That was fast." The assistant coach held the door open, almost getting run over in the process.

"Come on." Bree grabbed the poor guy by his arm and dragged him to the exit. "Hurry up. Unlock it."

Isaac crouched at the bottom of the door. "I'm going as fast as I can." He dropped the key ring, then had to find the right key again.

"I see headlights in the parking lot." Noah slammed his fist against the door.

"It's open. Go. Go." The assistant coach stepped to the side, almost cowering.

Noah sprinted toward the white Toyota sedan as it pulled forward out of the first row of cars. It turned right, and as Noah closed the distance, the kid looked out the side window, his terror-filled face focused on Noah's. Speeding past the curved sidewalk, the kid raced for the exit at the back of the lot. Noah cut through rows trying to keep up, but he was no match for a V-6 engine.

The moment the kid knew he was in the clear, he celebrated with an impressive backward skid-and-spin maneuver that Noah had seen in every *Fast & Furious* film, disappearing in a stinking cloud of burnt rubber and exhaust.

"Son of a—"

"Hey!" Bree slid to a stop at his side, bending at the

waist and resting her hands on her knees, breathing almost as heavily as Noah. "Get his plate?"

"84N, but that was all. Should earn us a few hits when we plug it into the system."

Coach jogged up to them in the parking lot. "Who the heck was that?"

Noah turned and gave the coach a penetrating look. "So, as far as you know, the school hasn't hired a new floor polisher?"

"What? Are you kidding? No way Bud would ever give up that job. He'd be lost without it. Told me so himself on more than one occasion." Coach tipped his head to the side. "Are you saying that kid was in the building, buffing the floors?"

Before he could answer, Bree asked, "Do you usually see the janitor when he does the floors?"

Coach took a few beats to consider the question. "You know, I used to see Bud pretty frequently, depending on my schedule and which part of the building he started in. But now that I think about it, I haven't seen him at all in the past week or so."

Something about this whole scenario with the kid didn't sit right with Noah. "You didn't recognize him? The kid?"

Coach shook his head. "Only saw him for a second when he ran past the exit door, outside of the building. But there was something vaguely familiar about him. Maybe the way he ran. I don't know, but it's right here somewhere." He tapped the side of his head. "Just out of reach."

Noah rubbed at the stubble on his cheek. "If you think of it, be sure to let us know."

"Of course."

"Thanks, Coach. And good luck with the game tomorrow."

"You'll be there, right?" Coach looked from Noah to Bree. "You should come, too. You ain't seen Texas varsity b-ball until you've seen the Resolute Roughnecks play."

She glanced up at Noah instead of Coach. "Ah, well, I'd certainly hate to miss that."

"Great. See y'all there. And good luck. Hope you find that guy."

"Oh, we'll find him." Excitement filled Noah's chest because he had a pretty good idea where to look now. Together, with Bree, they'd find the kid and solve the case.

It seemed ridiculous to be putting this much energy, this many hours, into such a petty crime. But he'd been assigned to it, and when Cassie returned, she'd learn how professional he'd been. How he'd followed protocol. By then, he'd have joined Adam's team, investigating the meth-house explosion. And after that, maybe—just maybe—he would finally be given his own case to run.

He was so close to reaching his goal, he could almost savor the sweet taste of success.

Bree reached out and touched his hand. "You know something, don't you?"

Her touch had been light, soft. Anyone else might have thought they'd imagined it. Not him. The hairs on his arms stood on end, and a chill raced through him that had nothing to do with the frigid weather. She stood so close, her breaths fogged the air he breathed, and her scent intoxicated him.

Lord, he wanted her. Not just her body. He wanted *all* of her. But he couldn't have her, and he needed to get that through his head once and for all.

"I know where our next stop is." He gave her his half grin that seemed to aggravate her so much. "Let's go."

BACK IN THE SUV, Bree massaged the back of her neck. "Hey, look, I'm all about chasing down a good lead, but it's past eight. You sure this overtime is approved?" Maybe, if they'd been working the meth house. But a school break-in?

Noah turned into a neighborhood. He must have a notion about who tonight's mystery floor buffer was. Something flickered in her mind, gone before she could grab hold of it.

"So, about that. How ticked off would you be if I un-officially told you that officially we're off the clock?"

"Dude, you are so going to owe me for this." Irritated at getting conned, she drummed her fingers on the armrest. "I'm thinking a Wagyu-steak dinner with all the trimmings. And of course, a top-shelf whiskey."

"Of course." That lopsided grin of his was back. "You drive a hard bargain, Delgado, but you got yourself a deal. Be the perfect time to introduce you to the Chute. Not sure they have Wagyu, but they've got the best steaks in Texas."

"Yeah, yeah, I heard all about the Chute and how

you Reeds like to initiate newcomers there." She sighed in exasperation. "I'm willing to go there for food and drink, but don't think for one minute you're getting me on that mechanical bull. And, Noah?"

"Yeah?"

"Before you play fast and loose with my free time again, you'll ask me, right?"

His grin disappeared as he glanced at her. "I should have this time."

"Yes, you should have. Lucky for you, I'm the forgiving sort." Bree craned her neck, looking down the street they were on. A few streetlights were out, making it difficult to orient herself. "Isn't this the same neighborhood where Rusty lives?"

"Good eye, newbie. Yeah, Rusty lives a few blocks that way." He hooked his thumb toward the passenger window. "Getting your bearings, eh?"

"Trying." Having lived in San Antonio her entire life, Bree could traverse it blindfolded. Although being geographically challenged around here hadn't been an issue yet, she'd hate to get lost on a call. "But the streets run at an angle inside Resolute, so once I pass the town limits, I have to recalibrate."

"And that's why we love our GPS." Noah slowed, then parked at the curb in front of a small, dark house and turned to face Bree. "Want me to fill you in?"

"Sorry, Reed." She tapped her head, much like Coach had done. "This brain is just way too fast for you."

"So enlighten me, Delgado."

"We went to the school to interview Bud, the floor polisher. Someone else was cleaning the floors, obviously on behalf of Bud. We're now parked in front of Bud's house to find out why he wasn't at the school, why he gave his key to someone else and who that someone was." She gave him a knowing smile. "Can we please stop wasting time now and get this night over with?"

"Don't blame me if you're smarter than you look." Noah opened his door.

"At least I can play the cute-but-dumb card when I need to." She met him on the sidewalk. "You know, when I have to hide my brilliance so as to avoid offending someone."

Holding up a finger, he stammered a couple of times. "This conversation will be continued later."

When she laughed, he headed up the front walkway with those ridiculously long strides of his. So *aggravating*.

"What's Bud like?" she asked before they knocked.

Noah shrugged. "He's, well, a different sort of person."

"'A different sort,' huh? Care to explain?"

"He has obsessive-compulsive disorder to some degree. He's also got social anxiety. Introvert to the max. He usually gets along fine with people he knows, but that's why he loves his job so much. He works nights— he'd never be able to be a daytime custodian in a high school."

Noah knocked four times and waited. When no one responded, he knocked four times again. The television voices they'd heard through the door cut off, and eventually a man Bree assumed was Bud Jenkins appeared. Midfifties maybe, a little taller than her, and stocky.

"Noah." Bud's infectious grin stretched across his face. He glanced sideways at Bree, then took a step back.

"Bud, this is Bree. She's our new deputy and works with me."

Bud nodded, glanced from her to the floor and back a few times, then kept his eyes downcast. And just stood there.

Noah poked her arm and indicated she should go on in. With Noah following, she led the way into an immaculate living room furnished with a retro '70s vibe. Yellows and greens. Gold shag carpet on the floor. Everything seemed worn and faded, but not a speck of dust or an item out of place.

"Okay if I sit on the couch?" she asked Noah.

He nodded, and they sat at opposite ends, Noah closest to a recliner. The sound of the front door being locked and unlocked, over and over, drifted in. Bree's stomach tightened, unable to imagine the impact OCD could have on someone's life.

The noise finally stopped, and with a shy smile and no eye contact, Bud crossed the room with an uneven gait and plopped into a well-used recliner.

Noah leaned forward, forearms on his knees. "I noticed you're limping, Bud. Did you hurt your leg?"

With his eyes occasionally darting to Bree, the older man focused on Noah. "Eh, it's sciatica. Hurts all the way down to my toes. Flared up a week or so back, and some days I can barely stand."

"Is that why you aren't at work tonight?" Bree asked.

He tapped a rhythm on the recliner's arms but didn't answer.

Guess I should let Noah handle this.

"I get it. It's hard to do all that walking if it hurts to even move." Noah leaned back on the couch. "You get someone else to do the floors for you?"

Sighing, Bud nodded. "My sister's oldest boy, Sammy. Told him I'd pay him, and he was glad for the money."

"Why didn't you just call in sick and let the school bring in a replacement until you felt better?"

"Last time my sciatica got bad, that's exactly what I did." Bud scratched his balding head. "Principal Jackson told me I couldn't be out that long again. And I just can't lose my job."

"By any chance, did you give Sammy your master key to the school?"

Bud's gaze dropped to the floor faster than a copperhead's strike.

"He probably needed it to get in, right?"

"Yeah. But I told him to be careful with it. And he's been doing a good job, he says." Bud raised his eyes, brows drawn together. "Something must have happened, or you wouldn't be here."

Bree couldn't take her eyes off Noah. Besides his lopsided smile and ridiculous jokes, he was just flat-out good with people.

"We just need to talk to Sammy. Someone broke into the school, and we're hoping he saw something that will help us."

"Am I going to lose my job?"

"I don't think so, Bud. I'll talk to Jackson myself if it's necessary."

That seemed to appease him. After collecting a bit more information and reassuring Bud again that everything would be all right, Bree and Noah left.

Back in the truck, they each made notes: Noah on the MDT, Bree in her notebook.

She sneaked a glimpse of his profile while he typed. As much as she hated to admit it, she hadn't been this hot for anyone in way too long. Her ex had been handsome, but his lack of morals, ethics and compassion finally revealed his true repulsiveness.

Noah was the full package. But she had too much on the line to risk taking things any further. No matter how appealing the fantasy, reality was seldom as rosy.

Shoring up her emotional fortitude, she looked up from her notes. "I see now why the sheriff wanted me to ride with you. This small-town, community policing thing is more complicated than I expected."

"You're catching on quick." Noah deepened his voice. "However, for now you are but the learner. I am still the master."

"The master of evil." She laughed at his shocked look. "What? You think you're the only *Star Wars* fan in this town?"

He clasped his hands over his heart. "Don't toy with me, Delgado. Because I seriously think I love you right now." Chuckling, he pulled away from the curb.

Bree chuckled, too. She had to because it was a joke.

Just another one of Noah Reed's lame, stupid jokes. So why had this one strummed a chord deep within her? Notes of happy promises joined with tones of painful loss, the poignant tune enough to make her cry.

But tears of joy? Or heartbreak?

Chapter Eleven

In the daily briefing the next morning, Noah assumed his usual position—feet up and ankles crossed on a vacant chair next to him, arms folded across his chest. He didn't mind the meetings. But once Deputy Dave got started on his daily manifesto of detailed *in*actions, imagined slights and unwanted opinions, Noah lost his patience. And today he'd been running late, so his infusion of extra-strong Busy B coffee still sat on a warming burner of the diner's Bunn-O-Matic brewer. It almost brought a tear to his eye.

He glanced a few chairs down to Bree, as he did in every meeting. Frequently. She'd gone from sitting erect and taking notes while Adam spoke to slumped in her chair, pen lying on her closed notebook. She caught Noah looking, and with a thumb hooked in Dave's direction, she smirked and rolled her baby blues until the color disappeared.

Good to know the newbie still didn't think much of Dave.

By the time the meeting ended and they reached Noah's SUV, the air had warmed enough to toss their jackets in the back seat. They swung by the Busy B for to-go orders but had to wait for Marge to brew another batch of Noah's special strength.

"Next time you're runnin' late, you better call me, or I'm gonna scrape that swill into a cup and make you eat it." Marge played musical burners with the coffee servers to open up a brewer space.

"Sorry, Marge. Would've been here in time, except Dave started talking and—"

"Say no more. I don't know where that man got the idea anyone wants to hear what he has to say." She hollered into the kitchen for the cook to hurry up. "Not much I dislike more than training a new cook. And this one?" She shook her head. "Just pitiful."

Noah peered through the pass-through at a twentysomething working the grill. "Where's Gus? He finally have enough of your cranky moods and quit?"

Marge smacked Noah with a menu. "The old man's fallin' apart. Had shoulder surgery and needs at least a month to recover. Probably longer." She leaned in toward Noah and Bree. "To be honest, I think Gus's wife got the short end of the stick. She has to stay home and rehab him."

Marge cackled, which got Bree laughing, which Noah approved of. It was a big, loud laugh. A nice laugh. A laugh he wanted to hear more often.

Marge pointed toward the kitchen. "But in the meantime, I'm stuck with Dumb or Dumber. Haven't decided which yet."

"Well, if it helps, my lunch here yesterday was excellent," Bree said.

"Club sandwich with fries?" When Bree nodded, Marge poked at her own chest, "That's 'cause I made it. Genius boy in there was out back on one of his many breaks. Claims the gas fumes irritate his asthma. More like the fumes he inhales on his own time."

When the extra-strong coffee had dripped its last drip, Marge filled Noah's travel mug and handed Bree a large to-go cup with regular strength. She pushed a bag against his chest that held breakfast sandwiches, based on the aroma.

"You two skedaddle. Breakfast's on me. Your sweet faces and laughter mean more than money this morning."

Noah gave Marge a peck on the cheek; then he and Bree left. They chowed down while taking Highway 111 north toward I-10. Adam had assigned them county-wide patrol duty all day but shortened it to a half shift when he'd learned about their burglary lead. With any luck, they'd close the high school case this afternoon and be ready for something new come Monday.

"Thanks again for agreeing to hold off on the search for Sammy until today." Bree sipped her coffee. "Last night, I was so exhausted, I barely managed to undress before I passed out in bed."

"Uh, sure." He stopped speaking, his attention wandering to a naked Deputy Delgado. He shifted uncomfortably, trying to bring his attention, as well as everything else, back to its original focus. "We'll track him down this afternoon."

Bud's sister's house had been their last stop the previous night, where they learned Sammy *didn't* live there. According to his mom, he crashed with friends, and his two younger brothers should know who. Noah had asked nicely, Bree had questioned more firmly, and the boys' mother had threatened life and limb before the two teens gave up the friends' names. They'd make those rounds when they got back.

As it edged past noon, Noah zigzagged back toward Resolute on two-lane blacktops. They pulled over a total of two cars, with Bree handling both stops. She wrote one speeding ticket, gave a warning for not signaling a turn and seemed completely at ease for the first time all week.

Her attitude baffled Noah. Nobody in the department enjoyed traffic patrol. It was boring. At least, he'd always thought so, and he couldn't imagine someone from a large urban environment not feeling the same way. But apparently, he'd been wrong.

Might be that she was an introvert and sought the solitude of patrol duty. She'd mentioned being used to not having friends, so maybe she was accustomed to going solo. Then again, perhaps solitude provided a barrier to shield her secrets.

Still several miles northwest of town, they came upon skid marks leading to a car on the side of the road. As they rolled up on the vehicle, Noah assessed the man bending over the open trunk.

Even in small towns, traffic stops came with an element of danger from the environment, the weather or oncoming traffic. None of that was an issue here. Or from driver hostility. The man straightened and gave them an inscrutable look.

"Stay sharp. Looks like a blowout, but you never know." Noah turned on his flashers and parked behind the old Chevy Impala. The man looked to be in his thirties and, based on the size of his biceps, someone who worked out on a regular basis. He also had what seemed like a nervous tic, bending his head to the side as if popping his neck.

Noah got an uneasy vibe and wasn't comfortable having Bree handle this stop.

Okay, maybe it was blatant sexism, especially since she had big-city experience, but he didn't care. His father had raised him and his brothers to be both respectful and protective of the fairer sex, and he wasn't about to change his spots to save anyone's sensibilities over the issue. Even hers.

"Run the plates," he said to Bree as he climbed out of the SUV, surprised when she raised no objection.

Noah walked up on the man with outward casualness. His hands rested easily on his duty belt in a nonthreatening posture, but one that would allow him to quickly draw his gun should the need arise. "Need any help?"

The man's mouth tightened into a thin line. "No thanks, Officer. Just digging out my jack. But I appreciate the offer."

Based on his dirty T-shirt and torn jeans, Noah would have guessed the guy had already changed his flat. But examining the trunk's interior, it looked like the man took care of himself about as well as he took care of his car.

What looked like a pile of rags, but might have been

more of his wardrobe, was balled up in one corner next
to a dirt-encrusted cooler. Fast-food bags, wrappers and
cups filled an old cardboard box and spilled over onto
the floor. Two plastic milk crates held cleaning supplies, everything from window cleaner, drain cleaner
and laundry detergent to toilet-bowl cleaner, dish soap
and bleach. A lot of supplies for someone who clearly
wasn't a neatnik.

The driver followed Noah's gaze and forced an in-
sincere chuckle. "Yeah, I need to clean it out one of
these days."

"Heck, my brother's trunk looks ten times worse
than that." Noah smiled as he told the lie, wanting to
put the man at ease. "You from around here?"

He leaned against the back of his car and crossed
his arms, and that's when Noah's radar started ping-
ing. This guy was trying too hard to appear unaffected.

"McAllen. But I just rented a house up near Hudsonville."

"Hudsonville is a real nice place. You'll like it there."

Bree approached in time to catch the end of the conversation. She gave Noah a small nod, which meant
nothing had come back on the plates. Still, he couldn't
shake the feeling that something was hinky.

Bree moved into a backup position several paces
from Noah. She must've ridden with a partner before,
because she did it smoothly and automatically.

"Moving to Hudsonville for work?" She took her
own casual peek into the trunk, though her right hand
rested at her hip, near her service weapon.

The man nodded. "Heard about an offshore oil rig that might have some openings."

While Bree talked to the man, Noah had made a nonchalant circle of the Impala. Back at the trunk, he said, "Your inspection sticker and tags are expired. I need to see your license and proof of insurance."

"Ah, man. You gonna ticket me right when I'm about to get my act together? I'm already going to have to buy a new tire. You know how much tires cost these days?" He reached into his back pocket, pulled out his wallet and handed Noah the documents.

He's cooperating and he's not belligerent, so why do I feel that I'm missing something?

"Jason Watson. Crescent Drive in McAllen. Your insurance is up to date, which is the reason I'm not going to ticket you." Noah handed the license and the insurance card back to him.

"Thanks, man. I appreciate that."

"I'm not going to ticket you, Mr. Watson," Noah repeated, "but when you change your address on your license, which must be done within the next thirty days, you need to bring your vehicle up to date on its inspection and tags."

"You got it, man. First thing. I swear." He seemed sincere for the first time.

"If you're sure you don't want a hand, we'll let you get back to it."

Jason nodded as he returned his wallet to his back pocket. "Have a good day, Officers. And thanks again."

Once back in their SUV, Noah activated the MDT and entered the house number on Crescent Drive that he'd memorized from the license. Bree had run the plates; now Noah would run the man. "What kind of vibe did you get from him?"

"I think he was lying about his job. Hudsonville seems a bit far from the coast for an offshore job he didn't even have yet." Bree pulled out her notebook. "So what set off *your* alarm bells?"

"And here I thought I was being so subtle."

"You were, but you have your tells."

"Remind me to never play poker with you." He chuckled, then grew serious again. "I can't say what bothered me about the guy. Just a hunch."

"Hunches are right more often than not."

Noah agreed. "I sure didn't like the looks he gave you."

"It's nothing I haven't seen a thousand times before. Part contempt, part lust." Bree looked up from her notebook. "Most of the time, guys like him decide a chick with a gun's not worth the hassle."

Most of the time. *What about the rest of the time?* A muscle-bound guy that size would have no problem taking down Bree. Of course, as she pointed out, Bree did carry a gun. But then again, maybe Jason Watson of McAllen, Texas, did, too. They hadn't searched his car. No cause.

The results on Mr. Watson came back. "Not even a parking ticket." Noah put the SUV in gear, pulled around the Impala and continued down the road. "What did you think about all those cleaning supplies in his trunk? Not exactly bomb-making materials, but it seemed strange, considering how filthy he was."

Bree closed her notebook and mechanically tucked it between her thigh and the car seat, leaving the little wire spiral sticking out. "What I noticed was everything in his trunk looked like it had been there for ages, but the cleaning supplies looked new."

"I didn't pick up on that, but you're right. Maybe he bought them to deep clean his new place in Hudsonville."

"Maybe, but..."

"But what?"

"For one thing, he had dirt under his fingernails and his hair was greasy. I doubt he's bathed in over a week. Seems hard to believe such a smelly, grungy guy is going to care if his windows are dirty or his countertops need wiping down."

A loud, gurgling rumble interrupted their conversation, and Bree laughed. "By the sounds coming from your stomach, I'd say it's lunchtime. Let's grab some chow and then go find Sammy."

"You're on." Noah took the next right turn and headed back to the highway. "It'd be nice if we could wrap up the school burglary by quitting time. Give us something to look forward to come Monday morning."

"You're talking about the meth-house case, aren't you?"

Noah shot her a high-octane smile. "Yes, I am."

Bree gave him a half smile in return, then turned her head and looked out her side window.

"Hɪ, Ms. Gɪʙsᴏɴ. How's your day going?" Bree asked as they passed Helen's desk in the lobby.

"Can't get much better than a slow Friday afternoon with everyone out of the office." The petite woman, whose hair was turning gray, smiled at her. "And for heaven's sake, call me Helen. We're mostly only formal in front of outsiders."

"Well, I sort of am an outsider. I've only been here—"

"Doesn't matter." Helen waved her hand. "Once you're working with us, you're family."

"God help her." Noah smirked. "Where is everybody?"

Helen checked her calendar where she kept track of all the office comings and goings. "Dave and Pete took over patrol for you two, and Adam and Shawn responded to a domestic dispute." Looking at Bree, she added, "One of our regular couples, south of town. They're usually past the point of reason by the time a neighbor calls us."

"We need to run a few searches, then we'll be out of your hair, too." Noah winked at her.

Bree laughed when Helen winked back.

In the bullpen, Bree copied the list of Sammy's friends from her notebook and gave it to Noah.

"I'll start from the top." He settled into his chair and tapped on his keyboard.

"Fine. I'll work my way up from the bottom." Walking to her desk, she looked over her shoulder at him. "Betcha I make it through more than you do."

"You're on." He typed faster. "What's the wager?"

"Hmm, I think I'll tell you after I win."

"In your dreams." He chuckled.

They pulled up names, searched for addresses, ages, records.

Bree liked her notes on paper, but she researched faster than most cops could turn on their computer. In less than ten minutes, she let out a whoop. "Five done, which means I win." She gave Noah her sweetest smile. "Would you like me to help you with your four?"

"Nice, Delgado. Hanging around with me is improving your sense of humor." He tapped a key and the printer whirred.

She picked up both hers and Noah's printouts and strutted to his desk. "And guess what's even better?"

"I'm sure you're about to tell me."

She waved the papers at him. "I've got an address for one of them."

Noah stood and read over her shoulder. "Oak View Apartments. Let's go."

Before they could take a step, his desk phone rang. He grabbed the receiver and listened to whoever was on the other end of the call for what seemed like a full minute before saying, "We'll take it." He dropped the handset in its cradle, a concerned frown on his face.

"What's wrong?"

"Have you got your notes from our talk with Bud and his sister last night?"

She retrieved her notebook and gave it to him without a word.

"Give me a second." He flipped through the pages, then cupped a hand loosely over his mouth.

As he handed the notebook back to Bree, a picture of Sammy slipped out from between two pages. His mother had made them promise to return it. He picked it up from the floor and gave it to Bree.

She'd been patient long enough. "What's going on?"

"I think Sammy is dead."

NOAH FILLED HER in on the way. A couple of kids playing by the railroad tracks east of town had seen a body. Male, young adult, dark hair. The general clothing description sounded similar to what Sammy had been wearing at the school the previous evening. Especially the T-shirt with the big red tongue.

"You think this somehow ties back to the burglary?" Bree asked.

"Could be coincidence, but—"

"I don't believe in coincidence." She crossed her arms.

"Neither do I. But I didn't see a single thing on the list of stolen items that would be worth killing for."

She tapped a finger against her chin. "What if we didn't get a complete list?"

Noah glanced at her. "You think someone's holding out on us?"

"More like something hasn't been missed yet. Something expensive." She shrugged. "We don't even know if it's Sammy yet."

"We'll know soon enough." Noah cut the lights and siren and turned onto a dirt service road running parallel to the tracks. They bumped along until he sighted a smaller dirt path leading into some woods.

He parked and climbed out, waiting for Bree, who

grabbed crime scene tape and extra gloves. The body lay in a small clearing surrounded by trees and bushes.

It was Sammy.

The clothes he'd been wearing when they chased him through the school matched what was on the body. But it was his face, the same face as in the picture his mother had given them, that left no doubt.

"Looks like he was strangled." Bree indicated the bruising around his throat. "Maybe if we'd kept looking for him last night, this wouldn't have happened."

"Woulda, coulda, shoulda. No point thinking that way." He pulled his phone from his pocket and dialed. "Helen, can you call the justice of the peace, tell him we need a body declared? Then contact Austin, ask them to send a crime scene team and a wagon."

As he put his phone away, Bree asked, "Y'all use a JP for death declarations?"

"Yep. Small-town life and all." He looked back at the body and grimaced. "Man, some days I hate this job."

Bree considered the area. "His car isn't around. He didn't come here on his own."

"He probably came with his killer." Noah studied the crime scene. "Or was just dumped here." He walked around the edge of the clearing, peering into the trees.

"What are you looking for?"

"I thought I heard something." He stopped moving and listened again. A rustling in the bushes made the hair on the back of his neck stand up. He spun toward the sound, pulling his gun.

Bree moved closer, her eyes huge. As usual, her head was on a swivel, but she had no weapon in her hand. Noah caught her attention, pointed to his gun and then to hers. She stared at him briefly, then indicated she'd circle around behind the rustling.

Why hadn't she drawn her gun?

He went in the opposite direction, planning to meet her halfway. Then they could push whoever was out there in toward the clearing. As he rounded a large tree, an odd sound began, along with more frantic movement. And then he saw it.

A female javelina with two babies. The mother, snorting and sniffing, found his scent and went into baby-protection mode. Noah raised his gun, intent on killing her before she went after him with her razor-sharp tusks.

And suddenly, Bree was by his side. Letting loose with a blood-curdling scream, she raised her arms above her head and threw a large rock toward the animal. The mama and babies took off deeper into the woods.

Noah gaped at Bree. "What the hell was that about?"

"Javelina usually run from loud noises, especially if you throw things at them." Her forehead creased. "You never learned that when you were a kid?"

"You know that's not what I mean." He narrowed his eyes at her. "Why didn't you pull your gun as soon as we heard the noise? It could've been Sammy's killer for all you knew."

She stayed mum and avoided his eyes. Like she was hiding something.

"I'm serious, Bree." It took every ounce of his control to not yell at her. "I want to know what's going on with you. Before everyone else shows up."

She lifted her head and squared her shoulders as if readying herself for battle. But when she spoke, her voice was almost a whisper. "I can't fire my gun."

"What?" Her words made no sense.

She stared him straight in the eye and repeated it, louder this time. "I can't fire my gun. I can't draw it, I can't fire it." She gnawed at her bottom lip.

"Physically?" Was that her secret? She was losing strength in her muscles or something? "Like, what? Arthritis in your hand?"

"Nothing like that." She combed both hands through her hair, leaving it tousled. "A while back, I shot someone. I was on duty, he had a gun pointed at me. It was a clean shoot." This last came out as if by rote. A memorized explanation, defending herself. "I haven't been able to pull it since."

"And Cassie knows this?" His by-the-book, rule-following sister had allowed this?

"No one knows. Except you, now." She dropped her gaze and kicked at the loose dirt.

He glared at her. "Does this have anything to do with why you quit your job and came here?"

Bree found a tree to lean against. "I did all the regular stuff after the shooting. Desk duty while they investigated it, which didn't take long. Saw the department shrink, who said I was fine. *Everyone* said I was fine. Ready to go back out."

She crossed her arms and seemed to fold in on herself. "But I couldn't report the gun…problem. They'd pull me from patrol, and that's what I live for. It's what I *am*. A patrol cop."

"So you decide to put everyone else at risk instead? Hell, Bree. You can get your partner killed if you don't have their back." He paced in front of her, fury pouring out of him. "You just put *my* life in danger. If that animal had been someone with a gun sneaking up on us... I can't believe you did this."

"I'm sorry, Noah. I truly am. I thought Resolute was a small town with little to no crime." She raised her hands, then dropped them. "I figured I could work through my problem while I'm here. Go to a gun range, practice. And I *can*. I know I can turn this around. I just need a little time."

He stopped pacing and stared at her. "You know I have to tell Cassie about this, right?" The past several days replayed behind his eyes. She'd impressed him with her powers of observation. Her attention to detail. And the whole time, she'd just been boondoggling him. Him and the whole damn town.

"Please, Noah, I'm begging you. Give me a chance, and I won't disappoint you." She pushed off the tree. "Please?"

"You've *already* disappointed me. I gave you way too much credit as a law enforcement officer." A bitter taste filled his mouth. "You played us all for fools, didn't you? Cassie, Adam, the whole country-bumpkin lot of us, right?"

She jerked her head back as if he'd slapped her. "I never thought you were a fool. None of you. That's not what... I didn't mean to..." Her tears flowed freely, and she spun away from him, her shoulders shaking in silent sobs.

Fighting the urge to comfort her, he crossed over to the far side of the clearing. "I can't promise anything right now."

His heart and his mind and his gut all threw down, each intent on winning this fight. He'd never experienced so many physical reactions at one time. Anger… when his father was murdered. Confusion…when his mother disappeared without a word. Care and compassion to this extent for a woman…this was a new one.

He sighed. "But I'll think about it."

Still facing away from him, she nodded her head.

He'd been right. Bree definitely had a secret. And now he had to decide what to do about it. As a responsible member of the department, he should report this to Cassie. If he didn't, would he ever be the deputy he was striving to become? And if he did, would he ever be the man he hoped to be?

He didn't want Bree to get fired. He didn't want her to leave Resolute. Because somehow, in less than a week, he was already falling in love with her.

Chapter Twelve

Despondent, Bree crawled out of bed Saturday morning and checked the time. Her appointment to look at rentals with the Realtor, Seth Whitlock, was in just over an hour. She straggled into the bathroom and gasped when she glanced in the mirror. Her sleepless night of worry and regret showed in the puffy, bruised crescents beneath her eyes.

Noah knew her secret. The sheriff, home for the weekend, would know soon enough. And Bree would be right back in the same situation she'd tried so hard to avoid.

She turned on the shower and stepped in, the cold water hitting her skin like icy needles. As if doing penance, she stood with her arms out to her sides, her face upturned beneath the frigid cascade.

Being a cop was who she was. She knew nothing else, wanted nothing else. She should have informed the SAPD brass the minute she knew she couldn't draw her gun. But that would've meant riding a desk, maybe for the rest of her career. And she'd heard the stories. Street cops didn't do well with desk duty. Some resigned. Some retired. Some ate their gun.

She'd chosen option number one, resigning—but with her secret intact, escaping to a place where she could work through her phobia with no one the wiser. Once she accomplished that, she'd return to San Antonio, or maybe check out Dallas, Fort Worth, Houston.

But she'd sure picked the wrong place to escape to.

It had been late when the last vehicle pulled away from the crime scene last night. And to say the ride back to the office to get her truck was awkward was laughable. Unless absolutely necessary, Noah hadn't looked at her or spoken to her the entire time.

She'd offered to go with him to notify Sammy's mother and brothers, as well as his Uncle Bud. But he declined, saying he'd prefer to do it alone. Which translated to: he didn't want to spend any more time with her. Or he no longer trusted her to work on the case.

As she dressed, Bree considered canceling. What was the point of looking at houses if she wouldn't be here long enough to rent one? But in the end, getting out of her motel room—and her troubled mind—won out.

When a knock sounded on her door, she paused just long enough to plaster on a smile. No reason this guy should have to suffer with a moody client.

"Hi. You must be Seth." She gazed up into eyes so dark, they appeared black. Flawless three-day stubble on his cheeks, black hair styled with care. His chiseled jaw and cheekbones made him perfect for modeling jobs, especially men's cologne or expensive suits.

Rachel had said he was good looking, and that was an understatement. But definitely not anyone Bree would be interested in. She gravitated to the rough-and-tumble type, jeans and boots, not afraid to get dirty. This guy probably showered three times a day.

"And you're Bree?" He flashed a white smile. "Ready to look at some houses?"

"Absolutely." She locked the door behind her and followed him to his car.

As they drove around Resolute, he made charming small talk, and Bree chastised herself for judging him based on his looks. She still wasn't interested, but Seth *was* a pleasant diversion from her dilemma.

"Rachel told me you flip homes?" Bree waited for Seth to remove the lock box from the front door of a cute yellow two-bedroom house. "Is this one of them?"

He opened the door and ushered Bree inside. "No, no. I don't have any flips available at the present time. A couple who moved closer to their kids and grandkids rent this one out. According to the property manager, it just became vacant last week."

Bree took the tour, which didn't take long. It was small, but she liked it. Close to work. Cozy inside, eclectic outside with flower boxes on the windowsills and a pink front door. A one-car detached garage sat off to the side, at the back of the lot with a long drive-way leading to it. Definitely an improvement over the Oak View Apartments.

By midafternoon, she'd seen several more rentals, was starving and still liked the pink front door house best. When Seth dropped her back at the motel, she thanked him for his time.

"I know which one I want, but I'd like to take the weekend to think about it." *And wait until Monday to see if I even have a job.*

"Of course. Just give me a call when you decide."

Inside her room, she flopped onto the bed and stared at the ceiling. *When I decide. Not sure I get to make this decision.*

Noah had mentioned that since the sheriff would be home this weekend, they had a family dinner planned for tonight. She glanced at her watch. He'd probably wait until after the meal to tell Cassie about Bree's *problem.* No point in ruining a nice meal.

Then again, there was a chance he wouldn't say anything.

Yeah, right. Noah was so focused on following protocol, of course he'd tell her.

Bree rolled over and rested her head on her pillow.

And he should tell her. Because her selfish, ignorant decision could have had dire consequences. Because one day, they'd respond to a situation where words wouldn't resolve it. Where a physical altercation wouldn't end with the guy in cuffs. Where a civilian's life, another deputy's life—*her* life—might depend on the one thing she was incapable of doing: drawing her service weapon.

The oppressive weight of guilt over that possibility threatened to flatten her. She couldn't live with herself if people who depended on her were hurt or killed because she froze.

If Noah doesn't tell Sheriff Reed, I'll tell her myself.

NOAH LINED UP four shot glasses and grabbed a couple of limes. "Nate, what time did Bishop say they'd be here?"

"He was kind of vague." Noah's twin filled one of the small glasses with top-shelf tequila. By the time the limes were in wedges, Nate had tossed his first shot. "He said he'd have Cassie here before the food was ready, 'glowing like a candle flame.' No clue what he meant."

Noah scooped the limes into a bowl and gave his brother a doubtful look. "Seriously, dude. How long has it been since you've been with a woman?"

Nate met his eyes. "Oh. Got it." He shrugged. "Bishop's a dweeb. No one wants to hear that stuff about their sister."

Just then, a blast of cold air blew through the house. The front door slammed, and a minute later, Cassie and Bishop walked into the kitchen.

"I bring you pecan pie." Cassie set one of the Busy B's delicious pies on the counter, tossed her purse and jacket onto a chair in the living room, and bellied up to the shot glasses.

Nate filled the four glasses while Noah handed out lime wedges. The saltshaker sat front and center. Bishop didn't drink, so he poured himself a glass of iced tea while the Reed siblings each licked one hand, sprinkled salt on it and took hold of their glasses.

Adam started the toast with the first word, followed by Cassie, Noah and Nate; then they all shouted the last word together: *"Arriba, abajo, al centro, pa' dentro.*

Salud!" They licked their hands, tossed their shots and sucked their limes.

"Y'all ought to take that show on the road." Bishop leaned against a cabinet, shaking his head at the family he was about to marry into.

"That chili smells pretty darn good, Adam." Cassie tried to sneak by him to sample it, but he chased her out of the kitchen.

Working like a well-oiled machine, Noah grabbed a tray of toppings from the fridge while his twin carried a cast-iron pan of jalapeño cornbread, and Adam brought the pot of simmering Texas chili to the dining room table. Adam ladled chili into bowls, and the rest of the Reeds passed the toppings and cornbread.

Meanwhile, Bishop sat quietly, his hands folded on his plate in front of him. Noah and Nate started spooning chili into their mouths. Cassie glanced across the table at Bishop, then glared at Adam.

"Where the heck is Bishop's dadgum dinner?"

Adam slapped his forehead. "Oh no, I forgot. He doesn't eat meat."

"Still," Bishop said with a smirk.

"I am so sorry. Let me go see what I can scrounge up for you." Adam disappeared into the kitchen, returning a minute later with a small cast-iron pot. He set it on Bishop's plate and removed the lid with a flourish. "Ta-da."

Noah leaned over to see the contents. "Looks kinda like chili."

"So here's what I did." Adam returned to his chair

at the head of the table. "As you all know, Texas chili doesn't have beans. So I took all the beans some ignorant non-Texan would've dumped in my mouthwatering chuck-roast chili and made Bishop his own little dainty pot of vegetarian chili. With no beer."

"Thanks, Adam. Very thoughtful of you." Bishop took a taste, his eyes grew wide and his forehead broke out in sweat.

"Even if it doesn't have beef, you gotta know it's gonna be spicy." Cassie winked at him.

"His might be a little hotter than ours." At Cassie's raised brow, Adam added, "I couldn't get the flavor in there with meat, so I added extra chilies."

"*Ours* has beer in it, right?" Nate waited for Adam's nod before eating more.

Noah poked his spoon in the air toward Bishop's food. "You can*not* call that chili, Adam. It's bad enough when people put beans in chili. But *all* beans? *No* beef? Uh-uh. That's not chili."

Bishop drained his iced tea and went back to the kitchen for more.

Adam glanced at Cassie as he scooped shredded cheese into his bowl. "How's the trial going?"

She swallowed a mouthful of cornbread. "I think it's going well, but I'm not supposed to talk about it. And even if I could, I couldn't." She took a sip of beer. "I can't be in the courtroom until they call me to testify. I've been sitting on a hard bench for a week, trying to catch snippets of gossip."

"You think they'll wrap it up soon?" Noah hoped

they wouldn't. He needed more time to think things through.

"For all I know, I could be there another week. I thought it would be within a few days." She shrugged. "What's been happening around here?"

"Well, a meth head trashed Sweets and Treats," Adam said.

"What?" Cassie set her spoon down. "Is Sandy all right?"

"She's fine. Deputies Reed and Delgado tackled the guy and brought him in."

"Really?" She smiled across the table at Noah.

"You don't have to sound so surprised," Noah teased.

Adam continued, "Yeah, they're quite the dynamic duo. While they had that guy at the hospital for his blood test, a mother brought in her young son, unresponsive. They were the ones who figured out he'd been exposed to toxic meth trash."

"Well, actually, Bree figured it out," Noah mumbled. *Just* have *to be honest, don't you?*

"What on earth is going on around here with meth?" Cassie asked.

"We're working on it." Adam leaned back in his chair and drank some beer. "Delgado knows a lot about drugs from her time on the SAPD, so when she and Noah wrap up the high school break-in case, they'll be joining my investigation."

Nate brought another round of cold beers for everyone but Bishop.

"Thanks, Nate." Cassie caught Noah's eye. "That

break-in sounded pretty minor. If Adam needs you two, why don't you just hold off on the burglary for now. There's a good chance it'll never get solved, anyway."

Noah pushed the chili around in his bowl. "You assigned me to that case. And I'm working it until it's done."

She frowned at him. "Come on, Noah. Don't waste any more time—"

"They're not wasting time, sis." Adam grimaced. "They just about had it wrapped up, and then their lead suspect was found murdered."

Cassie's mouth dropped open.

"So now they're working a murder investigation, which in the end might solve the burglary."

"Noah and Bree are working the murder?" Cassie's brows rose almost to her hairline.

"Yes, they are." Adam reached for another piece of cornbread. "Noah's been doing a great job, and I'm convinced he's ready for a big case. Especially since it developed from the one he was already working." He grinned at Noah. "He's been like a dog with a bone this week."

"I'm glad to hear that." She turned to Noah. "Sounds like you and Bree are working well together."

Bishop scoffed, then pretended he'd choked on a pepper. Cassie's gaze bounced between them before landing on Noah. "Is there something I should know about you and Deputy Delgado?"

Noah shoved a spoonful of chili in his mouth and shook his head. His brothers laughed. His sister didn't.

"Is working with her going to be a problem?" Cassie

scowled at him. "Because you need to stay focused on the job, not her."

"Lighten up, Cassie. I was just teasing him." Bishop shrugged. "Didn't mean to rile things up."

She set her napkin on the table and sighed. "I'm sorry. It's been a long, frustrating week." To Noah: "I know Adam's proud of you, and so am I. I asked you to step it up, and you obviously have." She rose, rounded the table and kissed him on the cheek.

"Thanks, sis."

"I haven't seen the new deputy yet, but I've heard she's cute." Nate gave his twin a mischievous smile. "What say you, bro?"

"Don't go stirring things up again, Nate." Adam stood and picked up the pot of chili. "While I'm putting this in the fridge, why don't you clear the table."

"I'll cut the pie." Cassie started for the kitchen.

Noah should help Nate clear. That was the deal. Adam cooked, they cleaned up. But instead, he remained at the table, pondering his dilemma.

Adam's confidence and Cassie's approval filled him with pride. At the same time, his dinner was burning a hole in his stomach, and not from the hot chili peppers. It wasn't in his nature to be deceitful, and the Reeds didn't lie to one another. But wasn't keeping quiet about Bree's secret a lie of omission? He didn't know what to do, and for once in his life, he didn't want to make an impulsive decision.

After fresh pie and hot coffee, Cassie and Bishop left, claiming exhaustion. Noah figured their excuse was close to the truth, since they'd most likely be spending the rest of the weekend in bed. Adam headed out for his cabin, one of a few separate buildings on the Reed property. Noah and Nate went into the kitchen to start doing the dishes.

"Seriously, what's this Bree like?" Nate rinsed off a plate and handed it to Noah.

"No leaks?" Their code for keeping their mouths shut. Like a pinkie swear for grown men who happened to be twins.

"No leaks."

"She's fascinating." Noah set the dry plate on the counter and took another one from Nate. "And you heard right. She's cute. And pretty. And smart. Riding with her this week has been great. But you heard Cassie—focus on the job, not Bree." His smile disappeared. "Nate, you have no idea how hard it is to be with her all day and know nothing can happen between us."

"Dude, life's short. Follow your passion. Whether it's a place, a job or a woman, you have to go for it, or you'll always regret it."

"Sounds like you've been hanging out with Bishop a little too much lately." Noah snapped him with the dish towel.

After they finished in the kitchen, Nate went upstairs to play a video game. Noah poured himself a small glass of sipping tequila and wandered into the living room. Sitting in his dad's leather recliner, he took Nate's advice to heart.

A week ago, he was already following his passion:

the job, pure and simple. Now he was torn between that and another, unexpected passion. A cute one with dark messy curls and crystal-blue eyes.

Which one should he follow?

Chapter Thirteen

A woodpecker hammered at Bree's head until she peeled back one eyelid and checked the clock. Seven thirty. On Sunday morning. The noise continued, but farther away. Someone at her door. Doc hadn't mentioned any early-Sunday maid service.

After Seth dropped her off at the motel yesterday, she'd summoned enough energy to pick up some takeout from a burger joint in town. She would have preferred one of Marge's, but Bree wasn't up to talking to anyone at the Busy B.

On the way back, she'd stopped at a liquor store for a bottle of wine. Just one glass to calm her had turned into just one bottle to forget the mess her life was becoming.

Crawling out of bed, she shuffled to the door and peeked through the peephole. Nothing but a wide expanse of T-shirt material. She closed her eyes, took a deep breath and opened the door.

"Morning, sunshine." Noah's voice ricocheted in her head, stirring up remnants of the wine hangover.

With one eye closed against the rising sun, she

squinted at him with the other. "What are you doing here?"

"Not a morning person?" He held a bag in one hand and a coffee carrier—with two large, steaming paper cups—in the other. "I brought breakfast."

She reached for one of the coffee cups, popped it out of the holder and closed the door in his face. After burning her tongue on the bitter brew, Bree took a quick shower, dried her hair, and dressed in jeans and a pink long-sleeve button-down. With any luck, he'd be gone when she checked.

She had *no* luck. When she opened the door again, he stood leaning against the SUV's hood, a half-eaten breakfast sandwich in one hand, coffee in the other.

"Good thing you were fast." He tossed the bag at her. "I was going to eat yours if you weren't ready by the time I finished this one." He grinned, then took another bite.

Her stomach didn't want food, but her hangover did. "Come on in. It's too cold out here." She led the way into her room and sat on her bed, leaving the uncomfortable desk chair for Noah.

Peering into the bag, she inhaled the glorious scent of grease, bacon, fried egg and cheese. As much as she wanted to just stick her head in the bag and breathe until he went away, she might as well find out her fate.

"What time do I meet with the sheriff?" Bree took a bite of her food, then reached for her coffee on the nightstand. She couldn't quite bring herself to look him in the eye.

"No idea. She thinks the trial may run another week."

"What do I do in the meantime?" Pulling her feet beneath her, she sat cross-legged and leaned against the headboard. "Desk duty? Or watch daytime TV in here, waiting for her to return and fire me?" She picked at the paper wrapper around her sandwich. "Why doesn't she just do it now, instead of making me wait?"

"I didn't tell her." Noah took a long sip of coffee, watching her over the rim of his cup. "Yet."

Bree's sandwich fell into her lap. "Why not?"

"I'll explain when we get where we're going." He stood and waited by the door. "Come on, let's go. Get your shoes on. You'll need a light jacket. It's cool this morning but supposed to be warm later."

Having no idea what was going on, she pushed her feet into her boots and grabbed a jacket. "Anything else?"

"Your gun and extra ammo."

She stopped in her tracks and stared at him. "Why?"

"You'll see." He paused, then added, "And you better make that *lots* of extra ammo."

There would be no point in asking him more questions, so she grabbed her gun and a canvas bag for her boxes of ammo.

Two minutes later, Bree put on her sunglasses as they drove east. She'd lost track of the roads and turns, and just enjoyed the scenery flashing past her window. After bumping over a cattle guard, they drove down a long gravel drive and stopped in front of a rustic two-story house.

"Welcome to Casa de Reed. I'll be right back." Noah left the vehicle running and dashed into the house, returning a moment later with two coolers. He stashed them in back, slid behind the wheel and they were off again.

"This is *your* house?" It seemed too big for a single person.

"My family's. Nate and I live there. Adam has his own cabin by the north end of the creek." He took a one-lane dirt road that branched off the large parking area.

"What about the sheriff?" *I'm not nosy, I'm curious.*

"She and Bishop live together in Cassie's house in town."

"Bishop's an odd first name." She held on to the grab handle as they bumped across a washboard section of road. "What's his last name?"

"Bishop."

Another one of his dumb jokes? *Okay, I'll play.* "So he's Bishop Bishop."

"Nope. Just Bishop." He glanced at her, lopsided grin in place. "His first name's Tyler, but everyone calls him Bishop. Something to do with when he was a kid."

A few minutes later, Noah parked in a wooded area and got out.

Bree followed suit, inspecting the area. "You're going to make me shoot tree trunks?"

"Close, but no cigar." He set up a wooden TV tray near a tree, then put a computer case on it. "Come on." He waved for her to follow him.

She tromped along behind him and his aggravatingly long legs. "Does all this property belong to your family?"

"Yep. My dad bought it and built the house before

he even asked my mom to marry him. She was artistic, loved nature, and he wanted to present her with a place she'd never want to leave."

Bree smiled. "And they got married." She loved a good happily ever after.

"They did indeed. They got married. Had four kids. And then she left."

She caught up to Noah and put her hand on his arm to slow him down. "I'm so sorry."

He lifted one shoulder. "Thanks, but it was a long time ago."

"How old were you?" Her heart hurt just thinking about four children being abandoned by their mother.

"Nate and I were eight. Adam was ten, Cassie eleven." Noah leaned against a tree. "Cassie got the short end of the deal. Dad worked a lot, so she basically raised us. Along with plenty of advice from Helen and a shoulder to cry on in Marge."

Bree stepped closer, rested her hands against his chest. "It amazes me how some people are such survivors. Instead of wallowing in self-pity, y'all just kept on going." She looked up into his warm brown eyes, captivated by the passion they held. "You're one hell of a man, Noah Reed."

"And you're one fascinating woman, Brianna Delgado."

She studied his mouth, the way the very corners curled up, even when he wasn't smiling. She'd thought about kissing that mouth more times than she'd admit, even to herself. But taking that first step—the one that could lead to so many others or to no more at all—was a complicated one.

Noah lifted a hand to her temple, his fingers brushing her curls in a way that was almost erotic. She closed her eyes and luxuriated in the sensation, trying to stay with it instead of wondering where his fingers would touch her next.

His other hand went to her waist, paused a moment and then slid to the small of her back. It remained there, holding her with just the smallest amount of pressure, as if to keep her from floating away from him.

There was no longer a reason to push him away. He knew her secrets. He knew things about her she'd never told him, because he'd watched her, studied her, *learned* her.

She opened her eyes to find him staring at her with an intensity that took hold of her entire being. His mouth was so close. And she knew. She was ready for that first step, to see if it would be the beginning of them or the end.

He cupped the back of her head with one hand and met her lips in a kiss that brought her to her toes. She leaned into him, delighting in every inch pressed against her—from the hard planes of his chest to his sculpted abs to his muscular thighs.

Sliding her arms around his neck, she hugged him closer to her still, if that were even possible. When the pleasure flowing through her body went far beyond their kiss, she pulled back, gasping for air. She rested her head against his chest until her breathing had slowed.

"I wasn't sure you…" he said, caressing her hair.

"I was." She straightened and smiled at him. "It was just so…"

"Complicated."

"Yes. But not so much, anymore."

THEY SAT ON a log, Noah's arm around her shoulders. He was trying to hold on to the kiss, the feelings, the sensations. But they'd come here for a reason, and he was determined to help Bree pull her gun.

"Tell me about what happened the day you shot that guy."

Bree leaned away and glared at him. "Wow. Talk about a mood killer."

He hugged her against him again. "That's what this day is supposed to be about. Getting you to where you can shoot again." He kissed her forehead. "But I want to understand the whole situation first."

"You want the short version or the long version?"

"Might as well take the long."

"When I was a kid, I started to get into trouble. A cop gave me a choice—get arrested or join the youth program hosted by his precinct." She snuggled a little closer. "I joined the program, it worked and I never forgot that cop. Fast forward, I'm a cop, I start a program through *my* precinct. One day, this kid walks in, says he's trying to keep his brothers from forcing him into a gang. He joined the youth program and stuck with it. Seventeen years old, college scholarships lined up, the world at his feet."

She stopped talking and scrunched her eyes closed. Her bottom lip trembled.

"What is it?"

Bree kept her eyes shut. "And I killed him."

He tried to wrap his other arm around her to console her, but she wouldn't let him.

"Just let me get this over with." She explained about the call she and her partner had answered for a jewelry-store alarm. Three men came out of the store—dark clothes, ski masks. They split up when they saw the patrol car. Her partner went after one; she chased the other two.

"When the two men suddenly stopped and turned toward me, they both had guns. One raised his at me, and I shot him. The other man hesitated, looked at the guy on the ground and then back at me. His gun was waving all over the place. He wouldn't drop it no matter how many times I told him to, and when the muzzle pointed at my chest, I did what I had to do." She paused, taking a deep breath. "When I pulled up their masks, I saw that the second guy was my kid from the program. Found out later that his brothers had threatened him to make him take part in the burglary. I *know* he didn't want to do it, because he was afraid of guns. Didn't know the first thing about them."

"Was his loaded?" He brushed a curl off her cheek.

Bree nodded. "But it doesn't make it any easier."

"And you haven't been able to shoot since then?"

"Every time I look at a target, I see his face. I can't even get it out of the holster."

"Well, why don't we fix that?" He kissed the top of

her head, pulled her to her feet and showed Bree why they'd come out to this isolated spot.

"What the..." Her mouth hung open.

"My dad wanted a shooting range on the property so he could teach us how to handle guns properly. But just plain old targets were too boring for him. Instead, he built this."

"A Hogan's Alley?" She walked from one life-size wooden cutout to the next, touching them in wonder. An old lady with groceries, a bad guy with a gun, a girl on her bike. And on it went.

"Before any of us could even start the process to become deputies, we had to ace the course ten times in a row. One miss, the ten-count started over."

"How do they work? Do you have to pull a rope or a lever on each one as I go through?"

"Originally, that's what he had planned. But Nate happens to be a computer genius. He moved up from video games to hacking and working on motherboards. I can't even explain the mechanics of it, but all I have to do is start the program. He's got them timed on some sort of continuous circuit, so once it starts, it runs by itself."

"This is unbelievable." She seemed lost in thought for a moment, then said in a soft voice, "Thank you for helping me. I hope I can do it."

The look of gratitude on her face reinforced his decision not to tell Cassie. And he hoped he'd never have to.

"Here's the deal. I'll walk behind you, keeping track of your hits and misses. You've got one week to ace this course."

Her face paled. "Ten times in a row?"

"No. Just once." He gave her a stern look. Both of their jobs might be on the line if she screwed this up. "One time through with no misses to prove to me, and to yourself, that you can have your partner's six when it counts."

The anxiety on her face morphed into determination. "Let's do this."

BREE DISASSEMBLED, reassembled and loaded her gun. Noah had moved the computer closer to the start of the course and carried extra ammunition for her.

"Tell me when you're ready, then I'll start the program."

She nodded, too nervous to speak. She kept wiping her sweaty hands on her jeans. "Let me practice drawing first."

"Okay. This is all on your schedule."

She shook out her arms, held her right hand near her gun and bent over with her hands on her knees. She was pretty sure her heart had stopped beating for a second there. Inhaling through her nose, she straightened.

Noah touched her shoulder and she jumped, some sort of squawk leaving her mouth.

"I'm sorry, I didn't mean to do that."

"Aren't you supposed to be back there with the computer?" She pointed behind him.

"In theory. But I don't need to be there until you're ready to start the course, and right now you can't draw your gun." His smile was sympathetic. "How about I stay up here and see if I can help you get over the first obstacle."

Bree tipped her head back, blinking fast enough to create a breeze. She was not about to cry because she couldn't pull her gun. Even if she *was* embarrassed, panicked and about to throw up.

Noah put his hands on the back of her neck and gently tipped her head down. "We both already know the problem, right? So why don't we both work on it?"

Nodding, she gave her cheeks a quick swipe just in case and shook out her arms again. "Do we have water in those coolers?"

Chuckling, Noah turned around and went to fetch not just a bottle of water but the whole cooler.

After a few sips, Bree was ready. She turned toward the course, and Noah stood directly behind her. So close, she felt his breath on her neck. It tickled. *Focus, Bree.* She brought her hand close to her holster. And froze. Then Noah's hand wrapped around hers, barely touching it. When she didn't move, he applied a gentle pressure, directing her hand closer to the gun.

"Take as long as you need."

His words in her ear acted as a spark. She touched the handle, then wrapped her fingers around it. As Noah took his hand away, Bree lifted the gun from her holster.

She put the gun back, turned around and hugged him. "Thank you," she whispered.

She practiced drawing it several more times, then worked her way to holding it in a two-hand stance.

"You know what?" Noah said. "Instead of starting with the course, let's try a plain old bullseye target."

"You think that'll be any easier?"

"You know this is all in your head, right?" He tipped her chin up so she looked him in the eye. "But the mind is powerful. So we need to catch it off guard."

"I'm not sure how to do that. Every time I think I'm making progress, I start hyperventilating again."

"Trust me." He retrieved an adjustable target stand from his truck and clipped a paper target to the two narrow side boards. After placing it in front of a small dirt hill that would catch the bullets, he moved Bree until she was facing it from a fair distance away. "Take your gun out of its holster and assume a two-hand stance."

When she was in position, he said, "Okay, that's just a piece of paper, right?"

She rolled her eyes. "Yes, it's just a piece of paper."

"It's a piece of paper that you can't hurt and it can't hurt you, so just shoot it."

Holding the gun in front of her, she aimed at the center of the target. Her hands trembled and her chest started to tighten. She placed a finger on the trigger and pulled.

Noah hauled her in for a bear hug. "Did I hit it?" Bree asked, still shaking.

"It doesn't matter. You shot your gun, and that's the only thing that does. Come on, let's take a break and have something to eat."

After spreading out a blanket for the picnic lunch Noah had brought, they ate and relaxed for a while, soaking in the sunshine amid a comfortable silence. Then they started another round of practice, continuing until Bree began to shake from the mental and physical exertion.

"Why don't we call it quits for today?" Noah said. "You must be exhausted."

"But I haven't even tried the course. If I quit now, I'll never make it through within a week." Her voice rose in panic.

"Let's set aside the time frame for now. You're making progress." He took her by the hand and led her to the blanket. "I've got some beers in the cooler. Want one?"

Bree collapsed into a sitting position. "That sounds good."

Bringing over two cold bottles, Noah sat beside her. "Here's to a day well spent."

"I'll drink to that." She'd been running on adrenaline, her emotions a roller coaster for most of the day. The icy liquid slid down her parched throat, instantly relaxing her. She leaned against Noah, and somehow the bottle disappeared from her hand and then he was kissing her. He held her, like he'd held her all day— supporting her, helping her overcome the biggest obstacle she'd ever faced. He cared enough to help make her whole again.

"I'm feeling a little more confident about my gun," she said when their lips finally separated. "But I can't quite put the moves together yet. Each thing is a separate, teeny, tiny step." She traced his lower lip with her finger. "Just like our first kiss."

WITH HIS ARM around her shoulders Bree lay back on the blanket, bringing him with her. He propped himself on one elbow and studied her face as if memorizing it. She would normally blush under such intense scrutiny, drop her gaze or look away. Instead, she reveled in being seen by Noah. She placed her palm against his cheek, shivering as her fingertips slid across its raspy stubble.

He kissed the corner of her mouth, her jaw, her throat, and she arched her neck, lost in desire. He fumbled with the buttons on her shirt with one hand, his lips never leaving her skin.

Threading her fingers through his hair, she gasped when her shirt began to fall open and his kisses followed his fingers all the way down to her belt buckle.

As the late afternoon's cooling air grazed the burning trail, she shivered. From the sensation. From anticipation.

Too impatient to wait any longer, Bree sat up, tugging her shirt free from her jeans. Noah gave her a knowing smile while her arms slipped from the sleeves and her bra followed. Then his smile vanished, replaced with an expression she'd never seen from him before and which made her shiver, her already hard nipples turning almost painful under the weight of his perusal.

But his gaze wasn't enough. She wanted his hands on her. On *all* of her. After pulling off her boots she stood and unbuckled her belt, meeting his eyes the entire time. Noah rose and toed off his own boots, then paused to watch her unzip her jeans, push them down her legs and step out of them.

In just her panties, she took one step closer and stopped inches in front of him. Her need to touch his body overrode all else and she pulled the hem of his T-shirt up. He took it from her hands and tugged it over his head, then tossed it on the blanket.

Where it fell, Bree didn't know or care. She was too laser-focused on Noah's well-defined chest and chiseled six-pack. Not overly bulked-up. Just toned and muscular. She licked her lips, reaching out with her fingertips to explore. As her hands moved lower he sucked in a loud breath, then released it on a shaky one. She inhaled the scent of his soap mixed with clean sweat and fresh air, growing lightheaded at the intoxicating combination.

With unsteady fingers she unbuckled his belt while searching his face for…what? A sign of regret for what he'd started?

But no. His warm brown eyes pulled her into their depths. He lowered his mouth to hers in a kiss that told her he regretted nothing. Then he unbuttoned his jeans and by the time Bree tucked her thumbs into her panties and slid them to the ground, Noah stood naked, his desire for her obvious.

She dropped to her knees, taking him in her mouth, teasing him. He held on to her shoulders, his grip tightening when her lips and tongue moved faster. Just as he tensed, he pulled out of her mouth and eased her down on the blanket to return the favor.

As his tongue and fingers worked their magic on her, Bree grabbed fistfuls of the blanket and arched her back, moaning as she came. Sailing on an orgasm afterglow, the faint sound of crinkling plastic drifted to her. Then Noah was entering her. Filling her. Making her feel like she'd found her new home.

WITH EACH THRUST, Noah felt Bree tighten around him. She'd driven him crazy with her mouth, but he belonged inside of her. Belonged *to* her. He'd been searching for respect at work, but what he'd really been aching for was a place of acceptance, a connection to someone, a home for his heart. And he'd found all that in Bree.

She was clawing at his back, calling his name. And every expectation anyone ever had of him faded in the moment, his mind and heart solely fixed on satisfying this woman. *His* woman.

Noah hooked one of her legs over his shoulder and thrust even deeper, making Bree come again. The pull of her around him, her fingers digging into his shoulders, set off his own orgasm.

This time they drifted back to awareness together, serenaded by the sounds of nature, cloaked by the lowering sun that filtered through the trees. And later they lay wrapped in the blanket, snuggled together while exchanging lazy kisses and tidbits of their lives until long after the warmth of the day had dwindled.

Chapter Fourteen

When Bree's alarm went off early Monday morning, she bounced out of bed, glad to be alive. What a difference a day—and Noah Reed—made.

She'd crawled into bed last night after a long, hot shower to soothe her aching muscles. She hadn't made it through Hogan's Alley a single time, but her anxiety and panic and adrenaline had left her body hurting. And then there were the good aches in other parts of her body. Those, she didn't mind.

Driving to the Busy B, she caught sight of herself in her rearview mirror. She sucked in her cheeks to get rid of the permanent smile on her face. The one that would alert the whole world that she'd had sex, it had been good and she wanted more. But each time her cheeks popped back out, the smile reappeared.

The whole world will just have to be jealous.

And the whole world began with Marge the moment Bree walked in the door.

"Morning, my little peach."

"Hi, Marge. How are you doing this morning?"

Marge peered at her and grinned. "Apparently, nowhere near as good as you are." She winked at Bree. "You must have had a fine and dandy weekend."

Trying not to care that her cheeks were burning, Bree shrugged. "It was okay."

"Well, I have a feeling Noah's weekend was okay, too, 'cause he's waiting in the back booth for you with the same silly grin on his face."

Her laugh followed Bree down the aisle. And Marge had been right. Noah sat with his back to the wall, watching her approach. And if her smile matched his smile, they'd be in big trouble at the morning briefing.

"Hi." She slid into the seat across from him.

"Hi." His eyes sparkled. "You look happy."

"You don't look so down in the dumps, yourself." She laughed.

"Sleep well?" Noah opened his menu and scanned it.

"Best in months." She dropped her gaze to her menu, cursing the butterflies in her stomach.

"Good morning, y'all." Rachel filled Bree's cup and topped off Noah's. "Ready to order?"

They gave her their requests, and before she left, Rachel said, "Sorry I couldn't go with you Saturday, Bree. Did you see anything you liked?"

Bree fought the urge to smirk when Noah did. "I did. A cute two-bedroom with a pink front door."

"Great. I'm glad Seth could help. Did you sign the lease?"

"Not yet. I'll do it later this week."

"Let me know when you're ready to move in. I'll come over to help." Rachel joined the smirk party. "And forget my kids there when I go home."

After Rachel left, Noah gave Bree a curious look. "You're renting a house?"

Bree nodded. "I looked at some Saturday. But I wasn't sure I'd be staying in town, so I held off on the lease."

"You'd leave Resolute if Cassie fired you?"

"I had no other reason to stay." She sipped her coffee.

His right eye twitched, a quick movement she almost missed.

"I see." He tapped one finger against his upper lip, a habit she was beginning to recognize.

"As of Saturday, I had no other reason to stay." She dropped her gaze, then looked at him from beneath her lashes. "As of Sunday, I have a great reason to stay, whether I get fired or not." *But please, God, don't let me get fired.*

The look of relief on his face zapped her heart like a defibrillator.

By the time they finished breakfast, they had a game plan for the day. Bree read it back from her notebook.

"After the department meeting, we'll get the forensics report on Sammy, assuming they're done by now. Then talk to his friends, see what they know."

"Or at least, what they'll tell us, which will probably be nothing." Noah leaned back in the booth.

She snapped her notebook closed. "Then maybe you should let me question his friends."

"You think *you* can get more info out of them than I can?"

"I guess we'll see, won't we?" She winked at him. "Care to make it a wager?"

"Darn right I do." His excitement was palpable. "If I win, you have to spend the night with me."

"And if you lose, *you* have to spend the night with *me*."

"You drive a hard bargain, Delgado."

"As do you, Reed. As do you."

AFTER THE MORNING MEETING, Noah went straight to his desk and checked his computer. "Still no forensics report on Sammy."

"Then I guess it's time to go find the boys and win a bet." Bree gave him a teasing smile.

He shook his finger at her. "No fair flirting."

She hooked her thumbs in her duty belt. "A deputy's gotta do what a deputy's gotta do." She turned and sashayed out of the bullpen.

Noah grabbed his jacket and rushed after her. He'd probably lose the bet, so he might as well enjoy the sashaying.

They drove to Oak View Apartments first, hoping to catch the friend who was renting there. With only parents' addresses for the other boys, they could easily waste the whole day running everyone down.

"This place is giving me definite déjà vu vibes." Bree peeked in her notebook one last time and stuck it in her pocket. "Just follow my lead." She got out of the vehicle and headed for the building.

She buzzed the manager to get in, like she had last time; and once again, it worked. She marched down the first-floor hall to apartment 116 and listened. "Voices. More than one here." She knocked.

A male voice came through the door. "Who is it?"

"Boone County Deputies Reed and Delgado," Noah answered.

"Hang on."

They waited about a minute before Bree pounded on the door again.

"I'm coming."

Locks disengaged, the door swung in and Noah stared at the new cook from the Busy B.

"Are you Lee Hayes?" Bree asked and waited for him to reluctantly nod. "Can we come in? We need to ask you a few questions."

Hayes's eyes ping-ponged between Noah and Bree. "What's it about?"

"Sammy Jenkins."

Hayes opened the door and let them come in. Three other men who looked to be in their early twenties were lounging on a couch and on the floor, playing a video game with the sound muted. Bree had each one identify himself.

Noah addressed them as a group. "Y'all know Sammy, right?" When they nodded in unison, he asked, "You heard what happened to him?"

A few mumbled responses, including from Hayes, indicated they had.

"We're following a lead that he's the one who broke into the high school." Bree looked at each of them, one at a time. "Is that true?"

"Yeah, he told us he did it." One of the guys on the floor spoke up. "Didn't sound like he got anything worthwhile, though. Pretty stupid, if you ask me."

"*Why* did he break in?" Noah asked.

"He never said." The kid on the couch lifted a beer can from the wobbly end table and drank.

Noah looked to the two still sitting on the floor. "Did he break into other places? Was this a regular thing for him?"

The only one who'd yet to utter a word shook his head. "Had to be the first time or we would've heard about it."

"Yeah. If he was proud of something, he always told us." This from the couch potato. "Like working for his uncle. No one was supposed to know, but he trusted us. Said he was making good money."

Hayes hadn't said a word since letting them in.

Bree faced him directly. "You knew he broke in?" Another nod from Hayes. "What else do you know about him?"

He shrugged and developed a sudden interest in the carpet.

"How's it working out at the Busy B?" Noah asked.

Hayes's head snapped up. "How do you know I work there?"

"Saw you the other day. Marge said you take a lot of breaks." Noah towered over him and used that to his advantage. "Marge is a good person. I hope she decides to keep you."

"Hey, man. I really need that job."

"That's between you and her. I just don't want to hear about you giving her any grief."

Bree turned back to the others. "Does anyone else have *any* information that might help us find the person who killed Sammy?" No one made a peep. "We're not interested in getting y'all in trouble. We just want justice for your friend."

"Thank you for speaking with us, Lee. If you think of anything else, call us." Noah gave him a card on their way out the door. "*Anything.*"

"I can't for the life of me figure out why anyone would kill Sammy." Back in the bullpen, Bree pulled the extra chair up to Noah's desk but paced around it instead of sitting. "Do you think it had anything to do with the break-in?"

Signing in on his computer, he shrugged. "Seems unlikely, since nothing that valuable was taken."

"That we know of." Bree stopped moving. "We never finished that discussion about how maybe something wasn't included on the list of stolen items."

Noah gave her a doubtful look. "If something was worth killing him for, why wasn't it worth reporting?"

Bree snapped her fingers. "What if it was something illegal?"

Again with the skeptical looks. "Like maybe a stolen piece of art, hanging on a teacher's wall?" He snorted and went back to his computer.

Bree sat and pondered the feasibility of her idea while Noah continued to tap on his computer keyboard.

"Finally!" He pumped his fist. "We've got the forensics on Sammy." He scanned his monitor for a moment, then read the information out loud.

"We already knew he was asphyxiated. But the autopsy indicates repeated strangulation attempts with a narrow piece of cloth. Hair and fiber's not back yet, but the marks and bruises are similar to those made by a man's tie." He skimmed parts of it further. "The repeated strangulation indicates the possibility of torture. Cutting off the air supply until the victim is almost dead, then releasing the pressure, reviving the vic and repeating."

"Maybe the killer wanted an answer and Sammy wouldn't tell him." Bree twisted a curl around her finger. "The fact that he was strangled instead of shot or stabbed makes it more personal."

"Could be the killer didn't have another weapon. Had to make do with what he had."

Bree nodded. "Or he didn't want to get bloody. Hard to explain to the family when you get home."

Reading more of the report, Noah said, "Holy sh… Listen to this. They found traces of meth on Sammy. Not like he used but was exposed to it. They found it on his fingers and inside his mouth."

"Maybe it got on his hand, then he touched a finger to his tongue. Like he wanted to taste it?" Bree pulled her notebook from her pocket. "Does it say if the meth contributed to his death?"

Noah ran his finger across his monitor screen, reading under his breath. "No. The report indicates it was diluted, so probably liquid meth."

Bree tapped her lip, then realized she was copying Noah's quirk and stopped. "Curiouser and curiouser."

Noah logged off and stood. "Do you have the phone number of Sammy's friend, Lee Hayes? The guy who works at the diner?"

She found it in her notes and read it to him as he punched in the numbers.

"Lee? Deputy Reed here. Are you still at home? We've got one more question for you. Okay. See you in ten." Noah ended the call. "He's at the diner. I want to ask him what he knows about Sammy and meth."

They made it to the diner in less than five minutes and waited out back in the alley. Lee finally pushed through the door, sat on an overturned five-gallon bucket and looked up at them.

"You and Sammy ever do meth?" Noah asked.

Lee's shocked expression seemed genuine. "I don't do meth. Smoke a little weed but nothing harder."

Bree took up a position next to Noah. "What about Sammy? Did he use drugs?"

His eyes flicked away. "I don't know, man."

"I think you do." Bree swung her boot against the bucket. "And this is your last chance to keep this here in the alley. Keep lying, we're taking you in for a proper interview."

Hayes blew out a breath. "I never saw him do any, okay? But I know he was friends with a guy who cooks meth."

Bree flipped open her notebook.

"Name?"

"He never told me his name. But he bummed a ride from me once when his car was in the shop and he couldn't borrow his mom's." Hayes looked up at them like a puppy hoping for a treat if he sat up and begged. "I think the guy lives on Mulberry. Sammy had me drop him at the intersection of Mulberry and Sunset.

He headed up Mulberry, but I drove away so I don't know for sure where he went. He could have doubled back to the intersection and gone a different direction after I left. Maybe that guy knows who killed Sammy."

Chapter Fifteen

"Somewhere on Mulberry." Noah scoffed. "He *thinks* somewhere on Mulberry."

They sat in front of the justice center, SUV idling, trying to decide what to do next.

"Well, it's more information than we had." Bree checked her notes. "And he did narrow it down with the cross street."

Bree had suggested driving around on Mulberry, see if anything caught their eye. But they couldn't knock on every door and ask if there was a meth lab in the house.

"Let's go in, run the property records for that section of Mulberry. Maybe we'll recognize a name." He turned off the vehicle and looked over at her. "If we come up empty-handed, we can always pick up Hayes when his shift is over. Drive him up there and see if he can pick out the exact house."

Bree nodded and they headed back inside.

Helen caught them before they made it past her desk. "I swear, this town's going crazy. Adam's tied up with another case, and he wants you two to handle a call that just came in." She handed Noah the information.

After he read it, he passed it to Bree.

"Another murder? Good grief. How many do you usually have in a year?"

Helen and Noah exchanged a look.

"We're reaching our max, and it's only January." The older woman studied Bree. "Seems like things have really picked up around here since you hit town."

Noah fought a smile as Bree narrowed her eyes at Helen.

"This isn't my fault. Don't even try to blame this on me. Nope. Uh-uh." Bree spun around, marched across the lobby and out the door.

"I better go, or I'll be stuck riding shotgun." Noah jogged after her.

The GPS directed them to an area southeast of town. Bree, as usual, had her head on a swivel, and caught Noah off guard when she gasped.

"That was Mulberry Street." Excitement made her talk faster. "When we're done with the body, we can check it out. I mean, we're already out here, so we might as well. Right?"

"Right." He figured it would be easier to humor her. But cruise around for the rest of the day, looking for a random meth house? Over his dead body. *Bad choice of words.*

After a few more turns, he parked on the shoulder of a narrow road. They exited the vehicle into a warm day with no breeze. Noah checked his coordinates again, then led the way to a grassy culvert and looked down.

The deceased lay partially on his side, his blank

eyes staring at the cloud-free sky. Noah and Bree stood there, not speaking, staring down at Jason Watson from McAllen, Texas.

BREE LEANED AGAINST their SUV, waiting for the crime scene techs to finish up. The justice of the peace had already declared Watson dead, then left in search of more pleasant JP duties. Noah was talking to a CSI named Brett, whom he knew. And Bree raked her brain like the sand in a zen garden, searching for any elusive detail she might've missed when they'd stopped to help the victim with his flat tire.

Noah joined her as the body was loaded into the medical examiner's van.

"This may not be a murder," he said. "My buddy Brett said there's no obvious signs of external trauma. But it did look like an overdose. We won't know for sure until the autopsy, but I'd prefer the OD scenario than another killer running around Resolute."

"Maybe this guy and Sammy are connected, and the same person killed them both."

"For now, let's just focus on Sammy. You wanted to go find his meth friend on Mulberry, right?"

"I thought you didn't want to."

"This call went faster than I thought it would. Might as well look while we're here."

She tried to appear nonchalant, like she didn't care one way or the other. But she had a feeling they'd find something if they just kept looking.

"Want to drive?"

Her shock must have shown on her face, because

Noah laughed at her reaction. But he had the same re-action as hers when she refused.

"I want to pay attention to everything while you do the driving." She hopped into the passenger seat.

Noah nodded. "Probably for the best. The way your head swivels around, you'd probably hit a tree."

"Funny." She powered down her window. "Just drive."

He backtracked to the intersection Hayes had mentioned, then crept along Mulberry. Bree practically hung out her window, taking note of everything she saw.

They passed the fourth house, and she'd turned to say something to Noah but instead yelled, "Stop!"

Slamming on the brakes, Noah looked around. Bree pointed behind his head, and he twisted around to get a better view.

"See it? Way back along the side of that green house? Isn't that Watson's Impala?"

Noah made a U-turn, stopped at the curb and they got out. Pulling out her small notebook, Bree compared the license plate number on this car to the one from last week with the flat tire.

"Same car, all right." She slipped her notebook back in her pocket. "Didn't Watson say he was moving near Hudsonville?"

Nodding, Noah circled the car and peered in each window. "We need to get a warrant to search the car."

"You think he lied about where he was moving to?"

"Either that, or he was visiting whoever lives here."

Noah glanced at the house. "We should knock, see if anyone's inside."

Bree wrinkled her nose as they walked back to the front porch. "This place smells...methy. I wonder if this is where Sammy's cooker friend lives, and Watson somehow learned he could score meth here. But that'd be quite the coincidence."

"Watson didn't look or act like an addict. I think he *is* the cooker." Noah knocked on the door and called out, "Boone County Sheriff's Department. Open up."

Lowering his voice, he continued to Bree: "And either he killed Sammy, or he knew who did."

"I'm betting he didn't do it. I think whoever did also killed Watson to tie up a loose end." Bree pounded on the door and repeated Noah's loud announcement to open up.

She stepped around a camping chair, set up next to a TV-tray table holding a coffee can filled with cigarette butts, and approached a large picture window. Curtains covered most of the glass, but in the center where they should have met, the two pieces of cloth fell away from each other. And through that gap Bree had a view across an almost-empty living room and straight into the kitchen.

"Hey, take a look." She stepped aside so Noah could view the scene. "If that's not a meth-cooker's dream kitchen, I don't know what is."

Noah moved away from the window, pulling Bree with him. "We had reason to knock because the deceased's car is on the premises. And the window next to the front door offered plain view of illegal equipment, including what looks like a drying oven similar to that taken from the high school chemistry room."

"And the odor of meth cooking was in plain smell, which usually holds up with associated items found in plain view." Bree smiled, satisfied with their findings. "Cover me while I check the other windows." Staying alert, Bree rounded the house and crept up to a window. Making sure Noah had her six, she tried to peek inside. The window was completely blacked out.

They circled the house; all the windows except the one in the front were the same. They approached the back door and listened. No sounds inside.

Bree tried the handle. Locked. "Wait a minute." She ran to their vehicle, retrieved their masks and returned, then handed one to Noah before she put on hers.

Once his was fastened tightly, Noah motioned her away and put his shoulder to the door. He threw his weight against it, and it swung in.

They walked into a small kitchen, cluttered with equipment and materials for cooking meth. After a look around from where they stood, they backed out and moved a good distance away. Noah called Adam, told him what they'd found.

Adam made it in less than fifteen minutes. After poking his head in the back door, he joined Bree and Noah by the back fence, an expression of amazement on his face. He made a call, and after disconnecting said, "Austin's sending the hazmat crew. Fill me in."

Noah explained about Watson, the OD and their previous encounter with him when he had the blowout.

Bree jumped in with the rest. "One of Sammy's

friends told us Sammy knew a guy in this area who cooked meth. We were cruising around, trying to find the cooker's house, when we saw Watson's car."

"Impressive job. Both of you." Adam nodded his approval. "I guess y'all wound up on the meth investigation sooner than planned."

"I'm not one hundred percent sure if Sammy's death and the meth investigation are connected, but they definitely intersect." Noah tapped his lip. "I feel like we're still missing something. Hayes said Sammy didn't do meth."

"I have faith we'll solve it soon." Adam clapped Noah on the shoulder. "You okay with taking charge here and waiting for hazmat? I've got a meeting with the mayor that I already canceled once."

Noah nodded. "No problem. We've got this."

After Adam had left, Bree turned to Noah. "Something's been tickling my memories since we found Watson. And it tickled harder when I went in there." She pointed at the house.

"When the hazmat team gets he—"

Bree didn't wait for him to finish. She picked up her mask and slipped it over her head.

"Bree, you can't go back in there."

"It'll only be for a second." She adjusted it, donned gloves, and ignored Noah's protests as she headed for the back door.

She went right to it and was back by Noah's side in seconds. She set the object at a distance from where they stood, pulled off her gloves and mask, and smiled in triumph.

"Laundry detergent." He didn't sound excited.

"Remember the cleaning supplies in the Impala's trunk? One of these bottles was in there."

Noah still didn't seem to make the connection.

She gave his brain a prod. "Remember the different brands of detergent in the gym's laundry room? Two of them were this brand." She peeled off her gloves, pulled out her phone and googled away before holding the screen toward Noah. "Which is only sold in Mexico."

Emotions flashed across his face: Confusion as he tried to make sense of it all. Realization about the soap bottles. Rage, most likely from a betrayal by his beloved Coach.

Chapter Sixteen

When Noah shuffled past Helen's desk Tuesday morning, her reaction to his disheveled appearance came as no surprise. Monday had been another long one, and he'd spent most of the night trying to put together the puzzle pieces of Coach, meth and murder.

"Good grief, Noah. Did you sleep under a park bench?"

"Good morning to you, too, Helen."

"If you're sick, you shouldn't have come in." Helen always had been able to scold and sympathize at the same time.

He scrubbed his hands across his bristly face. "I'm not sick. Just didn't sleep well."

"Hmph. At least you don't stink of alcohol."

"Gee, thanks." Since Cassie was still out of town, he went the long way through the building, stopping in her private bathroom to splash cold water on his face and finger-comb his hair. At least his clothes were clean, even if his shirt was wrinkled.

Looking a little better, he made his way to the briefing room and sat in the back row. He didn't want to talk to anyone this morning. Well, anyone except Bree.

The meeting was short, with Adam catching up the others on the new dead body and additional meth lab. Noah told Bree to meet him in Cassie's office. He wanted privacy for their discussion.

She showed up with two large notebooks, two large coffees and one large hug. The hug revived him more than the cold water had and more than the coffee would. They sat at Cassie's desk, the office door locked, and he began.

"We need to look at every possible angle on this thing before we take one more step." He downed half his coffee. "If we make a move on Coach and we're wrong about him, we'll both be leaving town on the next train."

Bree opened one of the notebooks and folded back the cover. "What did Adam say about it?"

"I haven't told him. I haven't told anyone." He leaned back in Cassie's executive chair. Their dad's chair before her. "What you have to understand, Bree, no one's going to accept our allegations at face value. I meant it when I told you before that everyone in Resolute loves Coach. We can't barrel in there and arrest him without any evidence."

She nodded. "Then we wait until everything's back from forensics. There has to be something they'll find. And then we'll have him."

He loved her for not arguing with him this morning.

"Let's start, shall we?" She handed him the other notebook.

While he jotted words and thoughts all over the page, Bree made orderly paragraphs and lists. They reviewed everything they knew for sure, beginning with bottles of the same off-brand laundry detergent—only sold south of the border—found in Coach's room, Watson's trunk and the newest meth house.

Bree looked up from her notes. "We don't know if the bottles contain meth. We don't know if the meth-house bottle was the same one from the trunk or an additional one."

"We have no proof that the bottles in the gym belong to Coach." Noah rubbed a spot above his eye where a headache was forming. "Anyone else with access to that area could have put them there. Including the burglar, who may or may not have been Sammy."

"As far as the connection between Sammy and Watson, we only have Hayes's statement that Sammy knew an unnamed meth cooker in the vicinity of Mulberry and Sunset." Bree sighed. "But we have Watson's car at the meth house, and hopefully we'll soon have his prints inside the house."

"But in the meantime we're assuming everything based on logic, which is the wrong way to investigate. Any lawyer worth his degree would drive a car straight through our case." Noah dropped his pen on the desk in frustration. "And I'll bet you my left nu…arm that there aren't any laundry-detergent bottles in the gym anymore. At least, not that brand. Which means Coach is free and clear."

In a low voice, Bree sang, *"Heeere she comes to save the daaay,"* while she fiddled with her phone. She rounded the desk with a self-satisfied smile on her face and thrust her phone in front of him.

Noah stared at a picture of everything that was in that gym cabinet the day they investigated the break-in. Including two bottles of their off-brand detergent.

"It doesn't prove our case, but it proves the bottles were there, and when." She pointed to the time stamp on the photo. "Told you I like to dot my i's and cross my t's."

Noah glanced at the locked door, then picked Bree up and kissed her like he'd never stop.

When Bree got her breath back, she said, "It still doesn't prove they're Coach's, but it proves they were there."

An hour later, Cassie's desk phone rang. Noah had told Helen where he'd be working, so he answered it.

"Forensics on line two."

Brett, a forensic investigator he'd met on a case last year, greeted him. "I'm sending you the reports, and you should have them within half an hour. But I know this is time sensitive, so I figured I'd give you a few of the results by phone."

Noah punched the speaker button and set down the receiver. "Bree's here, too, Brett. I put you on speaker."

"Okay. Before I forget, the autopsy report isn't completed yet, but they did run a tox screen on Watson. It was a meth overdose, like we thought."

"Okay."

"But highly unlikely it was accidental."

"You think he killed himself on purpose with meth?" Bree asked.

"He died from a large dose of one hundred percent

pure meth. Uncut." After a dramatic pause, Brett added, "Your guy was murdered."

Noah glanced at Bree, pretty sure his expression looked as surprised as hers.

"We also found contusions on his abdomen. We didn't see them at the crime scene because they were covered by his clothes, but they're large. We think the killer was kneeling on Watson's torso to hold him down while he injected him." A thread of excitement ran through Brett's voice. "But get this: the vic tried to fight back. We found quite a bit of flesh and blood under the fingernails of his right hand. Even had some under his thumbnail."

Noah couldn't believe their luck. "Tell me you got a DNA hit through CODIS." If the forensics team found a match in the Combined DNA Index System, this murder investigation would take a giant leap forward.

"Sorry, no hits. But at least we've got it and can test any suspects against it." Brett chuckled. "All you have to do is find someone with four parallel scrapes that are scabbed over. Easy peasy, right?"

"Right." Noah rolled his eyes. "Should have this case wrapped up within the hour."

"Maybe, now that you're working with Bree." This time Brett let loose with full-on laughter. "Anyway, I've got a little more info for you. The laundry-detergent bottle tested positive for meth. Apparently, mega-labs in Mexico make huge quantities of meth, but it's hard to get it across the border in its original form. So they put it into cleaned bottles of any sort and bring it across as liquid meth. Then the cookers on our side extract it from the liquid, dry it out and it's back to crystal."

"Wow." Noah already knew that, and from the bored look on Bree's face, so did she, but Brett liked to explain things.

"Next thing, we got fingerprints from the bottle. We ran them and got hits on a Samuel Jenkins; a Charles Crawford; and your dead body, Jason Watson."

Bree did a jump that made her look like a cheerleader for a law enforcement school. "That's it. That ties Sammy, Coach Crawford and Watson together with the bottle."

Noah was having a hard time containing his enthusiasm, himself. This was what they needed. But he had a question.

"Hey, Brett, where did the matches come from on Jenkins and Crawford?"

"Hold on for a sec. Okay, I've got it here. Samuel Jenkins. He was arrested at age nineteen for drag racing in Victoria County."

Well, that explained the tricky car maneuvers in the school parking lot.

"And Charles Crawford did a two-year stint in the army, starting at age eighteen."

"Thanks. I was just curious."

"No problem. And for the last fun fact, we got into Watson's phone. One incoming number was from a cell phone belonging to Cora Jenkins. So I'm guessing Mom paid for Sammy's phone." Brett chuckled. "There were also calls to and from a couple of burner phones. We don't have exact locations for them, but we tracked one to Resolute and one to Victoria. Both phones were purchased at the same store in Victoria."

"I didn't realize burners could be traced that well," Noah said.

"Well, we could only narrow it down to the cities. But it'll help in court if you happen to find the burners, especially in the possession of your bad guy."

"I appreciate the call. See you next time a body drops."

"See ya then."

"Do you realize what this means?" Bree paced circles around the desk.

"It means we've got a man to arrest. But first…" He grabbed her as she walked by and kissed her, leaning her back over his arm. When he righted her, she gasped for air.

"What was that for?" She fanned her face.

"That was for nothing. For everything. For being you. For helping me. For—"

Laughing, Bree said, "Okay, okay." She wrapped her arms around him. "Save the rest of the reasons for later." She tipped her head back until she met his eyes. "If you get my drift."

He leaned forward and kissed the tip of her cute little nose.

Her expression became thoughtful. "Noah? How do you feel about all of this with Crawford?" She patted his chest with the flat of her hand. "In here."

I feel mad, disappointed, betrayed…

"Not very good, but—"

"No, I mean, are you sure you want to be the arresting officer? You thought so highly of him, and he was your coach. Won't it be hard for you?"

"Community policing, remember? It's not always fun, but it's the job." He gave her a soft kiss on her forehead. "Let's go get a bad guy."

At 11:00 a.m., the basketball court was full of kids practicing their free throws when Noah strode past them, Bree at his side. Perhaps it was their posture, backs straight and shoulders set. Or maybe the Stetsons, which they rarely wore. But the laughter and joking faded away until the gym was silent. From the corner of his eye, Noah saw mouths hang open, eyes go wide.

He knocked once on the closed door of Coach Charles Crawford, then opened it without being invited in. They stopped at his desk, hands on duty belts. He wasn't sure about Bree, but Noah enjoyed watching the man's smile disappear, replaced by confusion.

"Hey, Noah. What's going on?"

"Charles Crawford, you are under arrest for possession and distribution of methamphetamine." Noah circled around the coach, who'd jumped to his feet, and placed cuffs on his wrists while Bree read him his rights.

Noah's vehicle sat double-parked in front, and they'd entered through the main school building. Bree had asked him if he didn't want to use the gymnasium door and keep it low-key. But Crawford's embarrassment didn't concern Noah. Meth in Resolute concerned him.

Exploding houses concerned him. Murdered young men concerned him.

The ride back to the office was quiet. Other than a few feeble protestations from the back seat that they had the wrong guy, no one spoke.

They put him in the cell next to Kenny, the candy-store destroyer.

"You ready?" Bree asked Noah.

"As I'll ever be."

They walked past the bullpen and knocked on Adam's door.

Chapter Seventeen

"Helen, I might be back a little late from lunch." Bree stopped at the older woman's desk, digging through her purse for her sunglasses. The cold snap had broken, the days now sunny and clear.

"Don't you worry about that. Half the office seems to forget their watches on Fridays." She cocked her head to the side. "Doing anything fun, I hope?"

"I'm signing a lease for a rental house. I want to get the paperwork done today so I can move in this weekend."

"I'm so happy things are working out and you're planning on staying." She leaned in. "I always hesitate to get attached to people, in case they wind up leaving. It's so difficult to say goodbye after you've become friends."

Bree grinned. "Well, I'm staying, so if you want to be friends…" She spread her arms wide.

"I'll take you up on that, Bree." Helen's phone rang, and as she picked up the receiver, she waved Bree toward the door and whispered, "Go get that house."

Driving through town in her own truck, she hadn't

wanted to take an official vehicle for a personal errand, Bree practically vibrated with excitement. Life was good. She had her job. She had Noah. And now she'd have a house.

But dang, this week was one for the record books. Adam had been livid about their arrest of Crawford. Once they'd laid everything out for him, he was only livid that he hadn't been informed in advance. But livid was livid when it was the boss.

Next week would be busy, too. They hadn't charged Crawford with murder yet, so that was on the agenda. It was easy for her to lay out a scenario where Sammy stole Crawford's meth and the coach killed the kid to get it back. But had he also committed the OD murder? Was he the only one involved, or were there others? Hard to believe the coach was top of the Boone County meth pyramid.

Enough! No more thinking about work until she was back in the office this afternoon. She lowered the window and let her hair dance in the breeze.

Turning the corner onto what was about to become *her* street, she noticed her Realtor's car parked in the driveway right in front of the garage. Seth was leaning into his open trunk and as Bree pulled in behind him, he looked over his shoulder, waved at her and turned his attention back to the trunk.

She joined him at his car. "Hi, Seth. Thanks again for working your schedule around mine."

He turned around, a binder thick with papers in his hand and a big smile on his face. The trunk lid fell from his fingers, and his smile faltered for a second. And then, as if it hadn't happened, the smile was back.

"Hello, Bree." He gave her a quick once-over. "I had no idea you're a deputy."

"Oh, that's right. We looked at houses on the weekend, and I wasn't wearing my uniform." She shrugged. "I'm on my lunch break today. I hope this won't take more than an hour."

"Nowhere near that long. A few signatures and you'll be back to keeping our streets safe."

He led the way through the house and spread out the paperwork on the kitchen island.

"Do you live in Resolute, Seth?"

"Me? No." He shook his head as he sorted through the leases and addendums in his folder.

"Well, I hope you didn't have to make a long trip today just for this."

"Here you are. One copy to sign, one to keep. After the owners sign, I'll forward you a copy of the fully processed document."

"That will be perfect." She started to read the lease, but part of her mind was wondering why he didn't want to tell her where he lived.

"It's a standard lease agreement for the state of Texas."

Bree glanced up from beneath her lashes. "Mm-hmm." As she continued to read, Seth seemed to fidget more. A couple of times, she caught him looking at her with a cryptic expression on his face.

She turned to the second legal page of small print.

"Would you like to take that with you, read it over

this weekend? We can meet again Monday for the signatures."

"Oh, no. I'm anxious to move in." She smiled. "But I do read contracts." *Especially when the other guy appears hopeful that I don't.*

The contract read like the ones she'd signed in the past, so she signed both copies and leaned over the deep island to hand one to Seth.

He slipped it back into the folder and pulled out another form. "This is the lease application. We don't usually bother with them unless someone is serious about renting. It's more of a formality, just to have on file. The owners don't have to approve you or anything."

He pushed it across the slab of granite, and the paper apparently hit a slick area. It shot toward her, Seth's hand still holding it down. His arm stretched out beyond the cuff of his long-sleeved shirt and Bree's eyes locked onto a row of four angry-looking scabs. The place where they started was farther up his arm, still hidden beneath the pale blue cloth of his shirt. But they ended just above his wrist bone.

Fighting the urge to glance at his face, Bree picked up the paper and pretended to read it. But the words and phrases flowing through her mind were: the killer was scratched, four parallel scabs, I need backup and how the hell did my Realtor end up being the killer?

She noticed a section on the application requesting personal information. She patted her pants pockets and lied. "I must have left my phone in the truck. I keep all this info in an electronic file. I'll be back in a sec."

He nodded as though glad she was wrapping things

up. But as she trotted to her car, her radar was already way past sending her *Danger! Danger!* messages.

She pulled her phone from her pocket as she walked between the two vehicles. Just before she dialed, she noticed his trunk lid hadn't latched when it slipped from his hand. She gave a quick glance toward the house; no windows along the wall facing her. Turning back, she opened the trunk. Two plastic bins of files and paperwork. An umbrella. And, partially covered by a bath towel, a box holding four jugs of off-brand laundry detergent, only produced south of the border.

Bree gasped and dropped the lid.

Does he know that I know?

She froze. A sense of something. Not a sound. Not a smell. The hair on the back of her neck stood on end. She reached for her gun and started to turn when her head exploded, blasting bright white light and colors and pain in every direction until nothing was left. And then, like a black hole in space, the nothingness sucked all the light and colors and pain and her into it, leaving just one final thought:

He knows.

BREE AWOKE IN the dark and assessed her situation. Pitch black, but no blindfold. The space itself was dark. A gag. Crunchy cloth in her mouth. Tape on her lips, pulling her skin. Sweet, rusty scent. Blood. Wet in her nose. Dried in the hair that was crusted to her cheek. Her head throbbed so much, she wanted to exchange it for a new one. Her ankles were tied together. Her wrists, too, behind her. She had no sense of time, of place.

But if she planned on living, it was time to leave.

Her extremities tingled from lack of circulation when she moved. She was on her side, so she tried stretching her legs out. Her boots hit a wall or some other obstruction while her knees were still bent. She wiggled her bound arms and body in the other direction, almost screaming in agony when her shoulder threatened to dislocate.

She could stretch full length moving that way, but the empty space was narrow. Rolling onto her back, she lifted her knees in a rocking move, gaining momentum. When her butt cleared the floor, she pushed her hands down and managed to get them past her butt and hooked under her knees before she blacked out again from pain.

NOAH LEANED INTO Adam's office doorway. "You seen Bree lately?"

"No." A frown crinkled Adam's forehead. "I thought she was working with you on the murders."

"She was, this morning. But she took off for lunch, and I haven't seen her since." He wandered into the office and took a seat. "She's not answering her phone, either."

Adam picked up his phone and pushed a button. "Helen, have you heard from Bree?" He listened, thanked her and hung up.

"She said Bree left at noon and was going to sign the lease for a rental house during her lunch hour."

Noah looked at his watch. "That was three hours ago."

"You think she decided to celebrate and just didn't come back?"

"She wouldn't do that." He stood, a growing panic taking over. "I'm going to go look for her." He left without waiting for Adam's approval.

At the bullpen's door, he asked if anyone had heard from Bree. A chorus of no's. Did anyone know where the house was that she was renting. More no's.

He stopped at Helen's desk and waited for her to get off a call. "Did Bree tell you where the house she's renting is?"

"No. But she was so excited about it."

The phone rang again and as Helen answered it, Noah left. In his vehicle, he called Doc's Motor Court and repeated his questions. Doc knew nothing, said her car wasn't there, but he rang Bree's room. No answer. Noah's anxiety grew.

He drove to the Busy B and double-parked by the back door. He passed Lee Hayes at the grill and found Marge by the front register. She hadn't talked to Bree lately, hadn't a clue.

Rachel squeezed past him with order tickets for Lee. "What's going on, Noah? You look like your dog died and your truck ran away with your girlfriend."

"Not the time, Rachel." Helen touched Noah's arm. "He's worried."

"I can't find Bree. Did she tell you anything about the house she's renting?"

"Yeah." Rachel yelled for Lee to grab her tickets, then pulled out her phone. "She said it was yellow and had a pink front door. I got the idea it was somewhere over near where Cassie and Bishop live." She held her phone in the center of the three of them. "It's on speaker. I'm calling Seth, the Realtor she used. He can give me the exact address."

When it went to voice mail, she ended the call.

Noah was already moving. "Thanks. I'll let you know when I find her."

He raced back to his SUV and started driving toward Cassie's while calling her cell. Straight to voice mail.

Dammit, Bree, where are you? A band was tightening across his chest. He didn't have time for a heart attack.

It's not a heart attack, you fool. You're in love with her.

He *was* in love with her, and he'd never even told her.

Noah punched Bishop's speed dial.

"Hey, Noah. What's up?"

"Do you recall seeing a house anywhere in your neighborhood that's yellow with a pink front door?'

"Yeah, it's one street north, two blocks west of us. Why?"

"Thanks. I'll call you back."

In less than two minutes, he'd parked in the street behind Bree's truck and pounded on the pink front door. There weren't any other vehicles near the house. Maybe her Realtor took her out for lunch and she lost track of time.

Nope. Something's wrong. I can feel it.

He drew his gun and kicked the locked door open.

"Bree!" he called.

No answer.

Noah cleared each room, continuing to yell her name. In the last room he checked, a small back bedroom—obviously empty—he paused. He'd looked in every room, opened every door except one. Fighting down panic, he walked toward the closet. Double folding doors, the knobs locked together with zip ties.

"Bree!" The door shook, and a muffled groan followed.

Noah holstered his gun and pulled his tactical knife. After slicing through the ties, he yanked the doors off their tracks. "Bree." He dropped to his knees and cradled her, pulling her into the room. He hardly recognized her with her face covered in dried blood, bruises and duct tape. But those eyes… He'd know those eyes anywhere.

He removed the tape with care not to rip her lips, murmuring to her the entire time, "I've got you, baby. I've got you." The rag followed the tape.

"Hur-ry. Coming back. Hands." Her voice cracked with each syllable.

Bent over her, he sliced through the zip tie on one wrist and was reaching for the other when she moaned an ungodly sound. He sat back on his knees and glanced at her face for no more than a second. Her eyes were wider than seemed possible, and as they bounced from him to behind him she wiggled her brows. The moan grew louder.

Thank God they could read each other's signals. He

slipped the knife into her free hand, pulled his gun and spun to face the monster who had done this to his Bree.

The man launched himself across the room and landed on Noah. They both fell to the floor near Bree, swinging fists at each other. Noah forced his way up to his feet until the two men leaned against each other like two evenly matched grizzlies fighting for dominance.

Noah surged forward and pushed the other man against a wall. He realized his gun was no longer in his hand just as the stranger headbutted him. Swinging away from the man, Noah spotted Bree struggling to cut herself loose. His gun lay on the floor next to her.

Damn. Wish I'd spent more time at the gun range with her.

The man charged him from the side, slamming Noah across the room. Noah kicked back with a foot, landing a hard boot heel to the guy's crotch. The man folded over in front of Noah, who grabbed his opponent's ears and followed up with a knee to his face.

Blood streamed from the man's face and Noah continued to pummel him. Then the monster within the man awoke once more. He wrapped his hands around Noah's throat and roared, blood and spittle spraying. Noah fought to loosen the man's fingers that were cutting off his air. He tried to force the man's arms apart to break the suffocating grip. He stretched his arms toward the man's face in an attempt to gouge out his eyes. Nothing worked.

Noah's lungs burned. His vision grew cloudy. Dizziness overcame him.

I'm dying. Bree doesn't know I love her and now it's

too late to tell her. But I can hear her voice. So soft, so far away, calling my name. Bree...

"Noah!"

Not so far away now. And definitely not soft.

Bree screamed, "Noah! Boot! Drop!"

Somehow, through the fog in his mind and despite the cryptic message, he understood. Noah swung his leg forward as hard as he could. Too close to hit the man with his boot, he put all his energy into his shin this time. And when his shin bone connected to the man's, uh, man bone, the fingers around Noah's neck loosened. The man pulled a gun from his suit coat pocket. Noah dropped flat on the floor. And Bree shot the monster.

"Good morning, Helen." Bree set a pastry bag with a prune Danish on her desk.

"Thank you, sweetie." She opened the bag and pulled out the sticky little pastry. "Who told you these are my favorite?"

"Must have been a little birdie." She gave Helen a wink and headed for the bullpen.

"Oh, wait. I don't think you've heard." Helen set the pastry on the bag and licked her fingers. "They got Crawford to roll."

"What?" Seth Whitlock, curse his black soul, had survived Bree's gunshot. And that turned out to be a good thing. With Crawford and Whitlock both locked up, there was a better chance of getting one of them to roll on the other.

"According to what I heard, as soon as Coach found

out he could wind up in prison with Whitlock, he sang like a canary."

"Awesome news, Helen. Thanks for telling me."

Helen waved a hand, her mouth already filled with sweet prune delight.

Bree set her stuff on her desk in the corner, where she now spent most of her time. *Coulda been worse.* Even though she'd proved she could draw her gun, when Cassie had returned from Austin, Bree held true to her word. She told the sheriff the whole story and awaited her fate.

Luckily for her, Sheriff Reed valued integrity and didn't fire her. Her punishment? Desk duty until she was cleared by a shrink and passed the Texas Police Academy firearms test. Small price to pay to stay in law enforcement, stay in Resolute, stay with Noah.

The aroma of Busy B coffee reached her, and she looked toward the door with anticipation. She just couldn't get enough of Marge's coffee. Or the deliveryman.

"Good morning." Noah set the coffee on her desk, took a quick glance around and locked lips with her.

Bree batted at his shoulder. She didn't need to worry about more reasons to get fired. "We can't do that in the office."

"Relax. I checked with Helen when I came in. We're the only ones here right now."

"Hear anything about the program?"

"Adam's meeting with the county council today. It's a slow progress." When she'd confessed to Cassie, her story included her youth program as well as her desire to start one in here. Impressed with the idea and initiative, the sheriff had started the ball rolling to create one for Boone County.

He gave her a smug smile. "I'm not supposed to tell you this yet, but my resourceful sister contacted a friend of hers from college. Sara Adams is a judge in Austin now. She came from an extremely wealthy family and inherited the whole fortune. And I guess judges make pretty good money, so Sara's philanthropic to the max."

Bree's excitement rose.

"When Cassie reached out to her about your program idea, Sara couldn't wait to jump on board. She told Cassie she'd make up whatever difference there is between what we need and what the council approves."

"Are you kidding? That's amazing. Your sister's amazing. Her friend is amazing. I just hope the council approves it."

"Don't worry. I'm sure if there are any speed bumps, Cassie and Adam will double-team the council and make the program happen."

"I hope so. By the way, I heard Crawford rolled." She took the coffee container with a large B on the side from the holder and opened the lid. "Helen told me."

"I wanted to tell you, but that's okay." He waggled his brows. "I've got all the details."

"Do tell." Bree followed him to his desk and dragged over the extra chair.

"According to Crawford, Whitlock was the local manager for this area. His boss's boss is in the cartel in Mexico." He drank coffee and turned on his computer. "Crawford was one of Whitlock's liaisons. He received deliveries and stored them, then dispersed them to the local cookers."

"Why on earth did he store them in the gym?"

"They had a routine set up. Whitlock would come to the gym on a prearranged day, at night when no one else would be there—but it wouldn't be suspicious for Crawford to work late. The coach also knew there were no working security cameras at the school."

Bree shook her head in disgust. "How convenient for him."

"He said at first he'd planned to move them. But they blended in with all of his laundry supplies, and it made him more nervous driving around with several bottles in his trunk. When he dispersed them, he only took one at a time and met the cookers in a private spot not far from the school."

"Are there a lot more cookers in the county?"

"Unfortunately, yes. But Crawford provided a list of all of them that he knew about. So unless we've got a few lone wolves out there, we should be able to collect the bunch."

"If they haven't all already moved far, far away." She reached over and straightened Noah's collar. "What about Sammy?"

"Guessing about parts of this, but Crawford thinks Jason Watson might have watched him leaving the school for one of their meets. Jason knew Sammy was doing the floors for Bud and told Sammy if he could grab a bottle, he'd cook it for the two of them. He most likely told Sammy to check in the science department for a drying oven."

Bree's mouth dropped open. "That was on the final inventory list."

Noah nodded. "So Sammy trashed the rooms and stole other stuff so the oven wouldn't stand out. And he faked the break-in so it wasn't obvious a key was used."

"But he wasn't smart enough to figure the back door situation." She sighed. "I'm almost afraid to ask who killed Sammy."

"Crawford. You and I actually put Sammy in his crosshairs. He said until the night we went to the school to talk to Bud, he had no clue who'd stolen his stuff. But when he found out the person we were chasing had been buffing the floors, and when he'd finally—" Noah tapped his head "—remembered what was vaguely familiar about him, it all fell into place."

"Are you going to tell me, or do I have to hurt you?"

Noah smiled his lopsided grin at her.

"What?"

"You just make me smile."

Damn, she loved this man. She hadn't wanted to. She'd tried not to. And she'd failed in the most fabulous way. The solitude she'd always craved now seemed impossible to endure, and she could only hope Noah felt the same way about her.

"Before Sammy dropped out of school, he was on the track team and had a distinctive running form. And since Crawford was responsible for the missing meth, he tortured Sammy until he told him Jason had it."

"Please don't tell me Crawford killed Jason, too."

"That was Whitlock, as far as Crawford knows. Said he'd told Whitlock everything up through who had possession of the meth, and Whitlock said he'd take it from there."

"You believe him?"

"I think so. It's up to the courts now." He looked around the bullpen. "I wish you were out there with me instead of riding a desk."

"Me too. But I will be, soon enough. And once I'm back in that car with you, don't think you're ever getting rid of me again."

"Like I would ever want to." Noah wrapped his arms around her and pulled her onto his lap. "You do know how much I love you, don't you?"

"I might. But it's still nice to hear."

"Then get used to it 'cause you'll be hearing it every day for the rest of your life."

Bree snuggled against him. "I love *you*."

"I know."

She punched him in the shoulder. "You do remember how that scene ended for Han Solo, right?"

Noah smiled his lopsided grin and kissed her.

Epilogue

"This girl needs no more champagne." Noah laughed as Bree danced around her living room. To help celebrate her release from a month of desk duty *and* her move into the new house, Noah had planned a party for her. And Cassie decided to add another reason to celebrate.

The entire sheriff's department, Marge, Doc, Nate—the whole gang was here. Casual dress was mandatory, except for Bree. Noah had managed to find a prisoner's uniform for the occasion.

When the music paused and Bree stopped dancing, Marge called across the room, "If I'd known horizontal stripes were so flattering, I'd be wearing them."

Bree pivoted like a model, rocking the prison stripes. The lightweight chain around her ankle, connected to a small soft ball, swung with each pose.

Adam sidled up to Noah. "She's a good sport for wearing the chain."

The zip ties she'd been cuffed with by Whitlock had cut deeply into her ankles and wrists, leaving noticeable scars.

"I know." He shrugged. "I left it up to her."

Helen carried a tray of appetizers from the kitchen and got stuck in a bottleneck next to Marge. Each woman's mouth set in stubborn lines, and they looked in opposite directions.

"What's up with that?" Bree appeared at Noah's side.

"What?" He pulled his best *what? where?* look.

She tipped her head toward Marge and Helen. "I've never seen either one of them ever look that angry."

Tapping his lip, he went with the first thing that popped into his mind. Actually, it had been on his mind all evening, so it didn't have to pop. He pulled her into a hug. "Do you know how hot you are in that uniform?"

"Nice try. What's going on between them?"

"We're not supposed to speak of it. Those that did, learned to never speak of it again."

Bree crossed her arms over her chest.

"Okay, okay." He pulled her to a quiet corner and whispered in her ear, "It's the oldest family feud Resolute's ever seen."

Bree gave him her questioning brow, the one he'd learned required an explanation or he'd have no rest.

"Helen Gibson and Marge Dawson are sisters."

"Get out!" Bree pushed him, and everyone in the room looked.

"Nothing to see here, folks. Carry on." He pushed his mouth against her ear again. "Do you understand 'do not speak of it'?"

Bree nodded with an adorable grin. "Why is it a secret? Why don't they talk?"

She'd never let him save the rest for later. "Marge stole Doc from Helen back when they were maybe eighteen or twenty. Something like that. Helen's never forgiven her."

Bree turned to him, leaning toward him from the waist, knees bent slightly. Her eyes were wide as dinner plates, her mouth open in an even bigger O. She looked like a bunny-slope skier who'd just hit a jump on a black run. He couldn't open his mouth without laughing, so he just held his finger against it in the universal sign for *keep your trap shut*.

He kept her in the corner until they could both compose themselves. "About that costume," he said. "Think you could leave it on after everyone goes home?"

"I think that can be arranged." She gave him her sexiest smile. "But now that I don't have any secrets of my own, I want to know *all* of Resolute's."

"Bree?" Cassie waved her over to the other side of the room.

"Hold that thought." She kissed him and disappeared into the crowd.

Noah moseyed over in the same direction, stopping at a table of filled champagne flutes. Helen called out for everyone to get a glass but not drink yet. Easier said than done with this crowd.

When everyone was quiet and holding a glass, Cassie stepped to the front of the room.

"I'm glad we all can be here tonight to celebrate Deputy Bree Delgado's release from desk-duty prison, as well as her move into this beautiful home."

Everyone cheered. A few tried to applaud, but…full champagne glasses.

"However, we're also here to celebrate another significant event."

"You and Bish are finally tying the knot?" Nate grinned as the whole room laughed.

"Very funny, little brother." Cassie's green eyes met Noah's, and the sisterly love in them almost made him cry. She motioned him up there, next to her. As he joined Cassie, Bree stepped to his side.

"I'd like you all to drink to the engagement of my brother Noah Reed and my soon-to-be sister-in-law, Brianna Delgado."

Noah retrieved Bree's diamond ring that he'd been hiding in his pocket until the announcement. He slipped it on her finger and they raised a glass to each other as their friends and family cheered, drank and applauded *after* they set down their glasses. Noah pulled her into his arms again.

"I was thinking," he said, "maybe after the party's over, we could head out to my place. Have a little competition at Hogan's Alley."

The corner of her mouth kicked up in a sly smile. "Bet I can get a higher score out there than you, Deputy. Even dressed like a prisoner."

He nuzzled her ear. Man, he loved this woman. "You're on."

* * * * *

COMING NEXT MONTH FROM

H HARLEQUIN

INTRIGUE

YOU CAN FIND MORE INFORMATION ON UPCOMING HARLEQUIN TITLES, FREE EXCERPTS AND MORE AT HARLEQUIN.COM.

HICNM0323

HARLEQUIN
PLUS

Try the best multimedia
subscription service for romance
readers like you!

Read, Watch and Play.

Experience the easiest way to get
the romance content you crave.

Start your **FREE TRIAL** at
<u>www.harlequinplus.com/freetrial</u>.